ONE OF THE POSSE MEMBERS CRIED OUT.

When Longarm looked in that direction, he saw the man toppling out of the saddle, clutching a bloody, bullet-shattered shoulder. Another man grunted and doubled over, hit somewhere in the body. Bullets were flying all around the men, buzzing like angry hornets. . . .

Longarm surged to his feet and lunged toward his horse. His hand closed around the stock of the Winchester sticking up from the saddle sheath. He hauled out the rifle and broke into a run toward a small gully he had spotted. It was about thirty feet away, and thirty feet was a long way when a fella was being shot at. . . .

When he could see straight again, he thrust the barrel of the Winchester over the lip of the gully and opened fire, blasting shots toward the slope where he had seen the sun reflect off a gun barrel.

jw 07-07

TABOR EVANS

LONGARM

AND THE ARIZONA FLAME

JOVE BOOKS, NEW YORK

LONGARM AND THE ARIZONA FLAME

A Jove Book / published by arrangement with the author

PRINTING HISTORY
Jove edition / May 2003

ISBN: 0-515-13532-1

A JOVE BOOK®
Jove Books are published by The Berkley Publishing Group, a division of Penguin Group (USA) Inc., 375 Hudson Street, New York, New York 10014. JOVE and the "J" design are trademarks belonging to Penguin Group (USA) Inc.

10   9   8   7   6   5   4   3   2   1

Chapter 1

The young woman was as pretty as a high country meadow full of wildflowers. She was tall and slender and her long, fiery red hair was piled on top of her head in an elaborate arrangement of curls. The dark blue gown she wore buttoned high at the throat and seemed sedate enough at first glance, but it was nipped and tucked artfully to reveal the elegant curves of her body. Her voice as she sang was low-pitched and throaty, with a hint of smoky passion in it despite the fact that she was singing the sort of sentimental, hearts-and-flowers ballads that her audience of rough, rugged Westerners ate up with a spoon. Longarm knew she was called the Arizona Flame because of her red hair, but he figured that she started a fire in the hearts of most of the men who came to her performances.

If he hadn't been in the saloon on business, likely he would've been feeling a mite combustible himself by now.

He wasn't here to listen to Glorieta McCall sing, though, or even to appreciate her beauty. He was after a bunch of low-down thieves and killers.

Glorieta finished the song, and the saloon exploded

with applause and enthusiastic cheers from the miners, cowboys, and townsmen who were packed into the saloon. The only hombre in the room who really didn't seem to fit in was sitting at one of the tables up front: a tall, slender, dark-haired young man who wore a short *charro* jacket over a white, ruffled shirt and tight trousers with colorful embroidery down the seams on the sides. The son of some wealthy Mexican ranchero from the other side of the border, Longarm decided. That guess was given weight by the presence of two hard-faced vaqueros at the same table. They were both armed. Bodyguards, more than likely, sent along by the boy's daddy to make sure that he didn't get in any trouble north of the border. As Longarm watched, the young man leaned over and said something to one of the vaqueros, who nodded.

Longarm himself blended into the crowd at first glance. He was dressed in range clothes: denim trousers worn outside his high-topped boots, a butternut shirt, and a denim jacket. His gunbelt was the same cross-draw rig he always wore, and so was the flat-crowned, snuff-brown Stetson. Most folks would take him for a drifting cowpuncher and grub-line rider. The ones who looked closer at his hawkish face, tanned to the color of old saddle leather and sporting a sweeping longhorn mustache, might decide he was an owlhoot on the dodge or, at best, a gent who made his living by selling his gun. The leather folder containing his badge and the bona fides identifying him as a deputy United States marshal was tucked away in a cunningly concealed pocket inside his saddlebags. Nobody in these parts knew he was a star packer for Uncle Sam, and Longarm intended to keep it that way for the time being.

He stood with his back to the bar as he applauded along with the other men. At another of the tables down front, an expensively dressed, sleekly handsome, middle-aged man with a narrow mustache came to his feet as he banged his hands together. The other members of the audience followed his example, giving Glorieta McCall a standing ovation. Longarm kept his eye on the man who had jumped up first. He had never seen the man before today, but he knew who he was: Jerome Horton, owner of the Southwestern Freighting and Express Company.

The saloonkeeper came on stage and hollered over the commotion, "Miss Glorieta McCall, the Arizona Flame! Give her a big hand!"

That instruction was a mite redundant, Longarm thought, using one of the words he had learned in his reading at the Denver Public Library. The saloon's patrons were still clapping and hooting to beat the band. Glorieta McCall curtsied gracefully, smiled, and waved to acknowledge the accolades. She started backing toward the wings, stage right. The audience wanted an encore. Glorieta made them wait, playing them like an expert angler plays a fish. She disappeared behind the curtains for a moment and let the torrent of sound build to a crescendo. Then, just as it seemed the noise couldn't get any louder, she stepped back out onto the stage, and the place went wild. She walked to the center of the stage, nodded to the slick-haired professor who pounded the ivories for her, and the saloon went dead quiet as the first tinkling notes came from the piano. Glorieta McCall started to sing again.

Longarm wanted to reach behind him for the half-full glass of Maryland rye he'd left on the bar, but he figured if he so much as moved while the redheaded songbird was warbling, the fellas in the audience would take him out and lynch him from the nearest tree.

So instead, he stood there and thought about the job that had brought him to Casa Grande, Arizona, in the first place.

• • •

Billy Vail said, "Silver and gold."

"Makes a man old," Longarm said.

"What the hell's wrong with you?" Vail asked.

Longarm shrugged. "I don't know, Billy. I reckon I just felt poetic there for a second."

"Well, stop it. This is serious business." The chief marshal harrumphed and pawed through the papers scattered on the desk in his office in Denver's federal building on Colfax Avenue. "The economy of the whole blamed country depends on silver and gold."

"All I know about the economy, Billy, is that I usually run out of money before the end of the month. Which means, as any pencil pusher could tell you, that you ought to be payin' me more."

Vail's balding scalp was usually pink. It got even more so as he glared across the desk at Longarm. "Quit yappin' and look at these reports," he said as he pushed some of the papers toward Longarm.

Longarm picked them up and scanned the words written on them. "Mule trains and wagons carrying bullion raided near Tucson and Nogales, Arizona Territory," he muttered. His expression became more serious as he glanced up at Vail. "Seven men killed so far."

Vail nodded. "Guards and drovers. The raiders hit those shipments and gun down anybody who even looks like they're thinking about putting up a fight. Folks down in Arizona Territory are getting up in arms about this, Custis."

"I don't blame 'em," Longarm said. He sifted through the reports. "Four bullion shipments have been hit so far."

"Yep. Each one a little farther west."

"Same bunch of owlhoots every time?"

"That's the way it looks. I reckon part of your job will be finding out for sure."

Longarm tossed the documents onto Vail's desk. He leaned back in the red leather chair and reached in his vest pocket to fish out a cheroot. When he had snapped a lucifer into life with his thumbnail and lit the cheroot, he shook out the match and started to drop it on the floor next to his chair.

"Don't do that," Vail snapped. "You don't have to listen to Henry bitch about it."

Henry was the pasty-faced young gent who played the typewriter in Vail's outer office. "I thought he worked for you," Longarm said, "not vicey versey."

"Sometimes you wouldn't know it to listen to him."

Longarm leaned over and put the match in the sand-filled, stand-up ashtray next to Vail's desk. He puffed on the cheroot for a moment and then nodded.

"I reckon my job's to head down to southern Arizona and put a stop to these raids."

"That's right. If the pattern holds up, the next place the gang will strike will be somewhere around Casa Grande. That's where you'll head first."

Longarm blew a perfect smoke ring and gazed on it with admiration for a second before asking, "Is there anybody down there I need to look up?"

"Gent named Jerome Horton owns the freighting and express company that operates those mule trains and wagons. Fact is, in one way or another he transports nearly all the silver and gold that comes from the mines along the border, either by mule train, wagon, or riverboat."

"Sounds like an important hombre."

"He's going to be a broke hombre if we don't put a stop to these raids. He's had to pay off on the losses to the mine owners."

Longarm's eyes narrowed in thought. "Any chance he could be mixed up in some sort of shady deal? He'd know when those bullion shipments would be coming from the mines, since he owns the company."

Vail shrugged. "I thought of that, but I can't for the life of me see how he'd be turning any profit holding up

5

his own company. You'll have to form your own opinion once you get down there, though."

"Reckon I'll keep it to myself who I really am, at least until I've gotten the lay of the land."

"That's up to you," Vail said. "You know I give you a free hand in these investigations, Custis."

"And I appreciate that, Billy. Now if you could just get Henry to stop bein' so dad-blasted persnickety about my expense vouchers . . ."

Vail snorted, as if to say that wasn't too damned likely.

Several days on the train brought Longarm to Tucson, where he had rented a horse and started drifting northwest toward Casa Grande. A stage line served the town, following the old Butterfield route, but Longarm preferred the freedom of being able to move around wherever he wanted to go. One of the first buildings he'd seen when he rode into town was a barn with the sign on it proclaiming it the property of the Southwestern Freighting and Express Company. That was Jerome Horton's outfit, he recalled from the reports he had read in Billy Vail's office. After he had taken a look around, he might decide to introduce himself to Horton and reveal his identity as a lawman, but not yet. Sometimes it was easier to turn over the right rock if nobody knew you were looking for scorpions.

He was just passing the barn, however, when the door into the office part of the cavernous structure was thrown open and a man stalked out, almost running into the big, buckskin gelding Longarm had rented in Tucson. The horse shied a little, but not so much that Longarm had any trouble bringing it under control. The man barely spared him a glance, muttering, "Sorry," as he turned to stride off down the street, his back held stiff in anger.

"Well, now," a voice said. "Looks like there's about to be a shootin' war."

Longarm had gotten that same feeling. He looked over at the man who had spoken, an old-timer who sat on the driver's seat of a big wagon hitched to a long team of mules. The wagon was parked in front of the open double doors of the barn, and it, too, belonged to the Southwestern Freighting and Express Company, according to the words painted on its side.

"You know that fella who was about to cloud up and rain all over somebody?" Longarm asked, inclining his head toward the retreating back of the man who had almost run into him.

The old man on the wagon leaned over and spat into the dust of the street. "I reckon I ought to. He's my boss."

"The manager of the freight company office, you mean?"

The old man shook his head. "Nope. That there was the big, skookum he-wolf hisself, Mr. Jerome Horton. Come up from the main office in Tucson 'cause he's got business with Campanella, the feller who owns the Golden Whore Saloon."

"The Golden Whore?" Longarm repeated. "Mighty strange name for a saloon."

"Oh, that ain't the real name of the place. It's really the Golden Horde, whatever the hell that means, but nobody ever calls it anything 'cept the Golden Whore. Except Campanella. He's a Eye-talian feller, and he can't figure out why nobody will call the place by its right name."

"You say Horton's got business with him? Freight business?"

"Well, yeah, the boss hauls in Campanella's liquor for him, but that ain't why he's come up here. It's got somethin' to do with that flamin' gal."

Longarm had taken up this conversation because he had learned over the years that garrulous old-timers were some of the best sources of information to be found on the

7

frontier. However, his head was starting to hurt a mite from all the twists and turns the discussion was taking. "Flaming gal? You don't mean a woman who's actually on fire, do you?"

The old man squinted at him. "What kind o' idjit do you take me for, mister? O' course she ain't on fire. It's all on account of her hair."

"Her hair's on fire?"

"No, it's red. You been out in the sun too long? Brain all addled from the heat?"

"I'm startin' to wonder," Longarm muttered.

"That can happen," the oldster replied with a sage nod. "It gets powerful hot down in this part o' the country. O' course, it's a *dry* heat." He leaned over on the wagon seat and thrust out a gnarled hand. "They call me Salty."

"Custis." Longarm shook hands with the man.

Salty had a short white beard and the sort of wrinkled, leathery skin that was mute testimony to a lifetime spent in sun and wind. The brim of his battered old felt hat was turned up in front. He wore a buckskin vest over a flannel shirt with leather cuffs, along with overalls and heavy work shoes instead of boots. His hands were big and strong looking, and Longarm was willing to bet that he had been handling mule teams for a long time.

"So who's the redheaded girl, and why's Horton all het up about her?"

Salty shifted a plug of tobacco from one side of his mouth to the other. "Name's Glorieta McCall. Ain't that a pretty name? She's a pretty girl, too, and sings like a damn bird. Better'n a lot of birds, if you come right down to it, since I ain't never heard a crow or a buzzard come up with anything 'cept squawks that was ugly as sin."

"What's Horton's interest in her?"

"Oh, I reckon he's sweet on her. She was slingin' hash in some Chinaman's place and sort of singin' to herself, you know, and the boss heard her and thought she was mighty good. He told her she ought to be singin' in some opry house instead o' totin' plates for a Chinaman, and she took to the idea just like he took to her. This was a few months ago. The boss sent all the way to San Francisco for some fancy singin' teacher—another Eye-talian feller—and brung him out here to give lessons to the gal. He figured when she got good enough, he'd book her into the opry house in Tucson, but Glorieta, she didn't cotton to that idea. She wanted to start off some place smaller, where it wouldn't be quite as scary. So Mr. Horton made a deal with Campanella for her to sing in the Golden Whore, and there you are."

"Not quite," Longarm said. "Why's Horton mad at Campanella now?"

"Oh, yeah." Salty scratched his beard for a moment, plucked something out of it, studied it, and then crushed it between his thumbnails. "Damn sand fleas. Anyway, the boss guaranteed Campanella would sell out the house, or he'd make up the difference, and now Campanella's gettin' cold feet. He knows the boss has been havin' some trouble, and he's afraid he won't get his *dinero* if the place don't sell out."

"What sort of trouble?" Longarm asked, making his voice sound only idly curious. He had started talking to the old man in hopes of finding out more about the bullion robberies. He'd had to take a long, roundabout route to get there, though.

"Owlhoots," Salty said. "They been hittin' the gold and silver shipments that the company picks up from the mines 'tween here and the border. They've grabbed off several of 'em, and the boss's pocketbook's been takin' a beatin' from it."

"Looks like Horton should be more worried about that than about some girl singer," Longarm commented.

"Oh, he's worried, all right. He's been howlin' to the law all the way to the territorial capital. But when a feller's all hot and bothered over a gal, ever'thing else plays second fiddle, even money."

Longarm grunted. "Maybe so. There any hanky-panky goin' on between Horton and this Glorieta?"

"How in blazes would I know?" Salty demanded, sounding somewhat offended. "That ain't none o' my business. She's been stayin' at Horton's house in Tucson, but I'd be willin' to bet ever'thing's on the straight and narrow. Miss McCall seems like a well-brought-up gal. Rumor has it her pa was some ol' desert rat who dragged her all over these parts while he was prospectin'. He must've kicked the bucket, though, 'cause she showed up in Tucson and went to work in the Chinaman's place. And now, Mr. Custis, you know ever'thing that I do. You're the most curious gent I run across in a while."

Longarm started to protest that all he'd done was prime the pump, but he didn't figure it would do any good. "I've been on the trail for a while," he said instead. "Guess I was a little lonesome for the sound of a human voice."

"I know the feelin'." Salty lowered his voice to a conspiratorial tone and went on, "Just 'tween you and me, there's been times when I was on a long haul that I thought these here mules would turn around and start to talk to me."

Longarm didn't doubt that a bit.

"You know anything about the gang that's been pulling off those robberies?" he asked, still trying not to sound overly inquisitive.

Salty spat again and shook his head. "Nary a thing. I been lucky enough not to be on any o' the runs that got hit. I lost a couple o' good friends to them no-good, thievin' rapscallions, though. Drivers I've knowed for nigh on to twenty years."

"Well, I imagine the law will catch up to the robbers sooner or later."

The old man snorted in contempt. "The law! Down here

in this corner o' the territory, the only real law is what a man packs on his hip. I see you've thrown a little lead yourself in your time."

Longarm frowned. "What makes you think that?"

"That fast-draw rig you're sportin'. That's a gunslinger's outfit, ain't it?"

Longarm just shrugged, willing to let Salty think whatever he wanted to. "It's comfortable for me, that's all I can say."

"Well, all I can say is you best watch yourself while you're in Casa Grande. There's a heap o' bad hombres in these parts, or some that think they're bad, anyway, and most of 'em are always lookin' to make a rep for themselves by gunnin' somebody down."

"I'll remember that," Longarm promised. "I'm not lookin' for trouble."

"You don't have to go lookin' for it. It'll find you."

Longarm knew the feeling. He nodded to Salty, said, "See you around," and walked his horse on down the street. He passed the Golden Horde Saloon and saw a placard on the boardwalk in front announcing that the beautiful Miss Glorieta McCall, the world famous Arizona Flame, would be performing there for one night only. Longarm didn't know about the beautiful part, since he hadn't yet seen Glorieta McCall, but considering that this was to be her first performance, he didn't see how she could be world famous. Maybe she was good enough that she soon would be, though he wasn't sure that would be the case. If Jerome Horton was as smitten with her as Salty had said, it was entirely possible that she was a terrible singer and Horton was only playing up to her to get her into his bed.

On impulse, Longarm reined in and swung down from the saddle, looping the buckskin's reins over one of the hitch rails in front of the saloon. He stepped up to the boardwalk and pushed through the batwings. The Golden

Horde was fancy enough on the inside, with a long hard-wood bar, crystal chandeliers, an elaborate gambling lay-out, and a good-sized stage with purple curtains at the far end of the big room. That was where Glorieta McCall would perform, Longarm supposed.

Quite a few customers were in the saloon, some stand-ing at the bar, some sitting at tables with girls in short, spangled dresses, and others playing poker, roulette, or bucking the tiger at faro. Longarm found an open spot at the bar and ordered a beer from a balding, red-faced drink juggler. He looked around the room for Jerome Horton but didn't see any sign of the freight company owner. If Horton was wrangling with the saloon owner, Campa-nella, they must have been having their argument behind closed doors.

"Say," Longarm said to the bartender after sipping his beer and finding it surprisingly cold and good, "what're the chances of buyin' a ticket for the show you're havin' here tonight?"

"Sure, I think there are still a few left. Looks like it's going to be a sellout, though."

That ought to ease Campanella's mind, Longarm thought, and cause one less worry for Horton. The ticket wasn't cheap—a whole six bits—but he dug out the coins and slid them across the bar, along with another two bits to pay for the beer. The bartender gave him a slip of paper printed in gaudy colors. "Hang on to that," the man ad-vised. "You'll need it to get in."

"Much obliged, old son. I ain't seen a good show in quite a while."

"Better get here early. The place is liable to be crowded."

And so it was. Longarm had checked in at a decidedly non-fancy but clean hotel down the street, washed off the trail dust, put on a clean shirt, and returned to the Golden Horde as night was falling. He'd had to surrender his ticket at the door to a burly gent whose nose had been broken more than once in the past. Platters of friend chicken legs, pickles, and hard-boiled eggs were set out on the bar, free for the taking, so he'd made supper on that and washed down the food with several more mugs of cold beer. He'd switched to Maryland rye before the show started, though. Somehow it seemed more appropriate.

Now Glorieta McCall was about to finish her encore, and the audience was as rapt as ever. Longarm told himself he was there just to keep an eye on Horton, but he had to admit to himself that he had enjoyed Glorieta's performance. She was beautiful, no doubt about that, and she could sing, to boot. She was talented enough that maybe someday she *would* be world famous. In the meantime, Horton had himself a pretty gal to take his mind off his current troubles.

When the song was over, Glorieta curtsied her way offstage to the accompaniment of just as much applause and whistling and shouting as had followed the first part of her performance. Horton was on his feet again, leading the standing ovation.

A few tables away, the rich, young, Mexican stuck his fingers in his mouth and let out a piercing whistle. Horton glanced over at him and didn't appear to be too happy. Horton had to be pleased overall that his protégée's performance had gone so well, but maybe he was getting a little jealous because of the reactions she had provoked. Longarm didn't really care one way or the other how Horton was feeling. He was just interested in finding out whatever he could about the man whose company had been the victim of the bullion robberies.

Suddenly, the young grandee left his table and started toward the door that led backstage. Longarm saw Horton turn quickly and call something to Campanella. The room was too full of noise for Longarm to make out what Hor-

13

ton said. But Campanella reacted immediately, motioning to the big gent with the much-broken nose, who was standing against the opposite wall. That fella moved over to block the young Mexican's way, and one of the vaquero bodyguards surged forward, hand dropping to his gun butt. The other bodyguard was no longer at the table; he had slipped out sometime without Longarm noticing. Most of the men in the room weren't aware of the trouble developing, but Longarm knew that unless something happened mighty quickly, there was going to be a ruckus, maybe even gunplay.

Instead, the applause stopped short and a stunned silence fell on the room, broken only by the frightened screams coming from backstage.

Coming from Glorieta McCall.

Chapter 2

The voice that had been lifted in beautiful song mere minutes before now sounded terrified. The hush inside the saloon lasted only a second, and then all hell broke loose. Most of the men in the place rushed the stage, anxious to get back there and rescue Glorieta McCall from whatever—or whoever—was after her.

Longarm reacted differently, wheeling away from the bar and starting toward the front of the saloon. It stood to reason that there would be a back door into the building, and odds were he could reach it quicker by going around than he could by trying to force his way through the crowd of men clogging the area in front of the stage.

He slapped the batwings aside and ran out onto the boardwalk, turning toward the alley alongside the Golden Horde. It was dark in the alley, and he hoped he wouldn't trip over anything. He didn't let that slow him down, however. As he plunged through the shadows toward the rear of the building, the stygian gloom suddenly was split by light spilling out from a door that had just been thrown open. Several struggling figures staggered out into the alley.

"Hey!" Longarm yelled as he palmed out his Colt. "Let go of her!"

He could see now that there were two men at the end of the alley, fighting with Glorieta McCall as they tried to drag her away from the building. One of the men had his hand clamped over her mouth, stifling her screams. The other would-be kidnapper let go of Glorieta's arm and spun toward Longarm. His hand came up with a gun in it.

Longarm hesitated. He was a good shot, but the girl was right behind the man with the gun. Longarm knew that if he fired and missed, there was a good chance he'd hit Glorieta. He couldn't take that risk.

But he couldn't just stand there and let that gun-toting hombre shoot him, either. He dove forward, landing on some sort of foul-smelling muck, as Colt flame bloomed in the darkness. The bullet whipped through the air above his head, about where his belly had been a second earlier. Lying prone, Longarm risked a shot. He aimed at the gun-man's legs as he fired and was rewarded by a howl of pain as the man toppled over. Even with a leg shot out from under him, the gunman still was dangerous. He crawled toward Longarm, firing as he came. Longarm rolled to the side of the alley and wound up behind a rain barrel. Thrusting his gun out from behind the cover of the barrel, he slammed two more shots at the fallen gunman and saw the man shudder and roll over onto his back.

Meanwhile, a few feet away, Glorieta McCall was still trying to escape from the other kidnapper. The man yelped and jerked his hand away from her mouth, and Longarm figured she had bitten the hell out of him. That also loosened his grip enough so that she was able to pull away from him. She threw herself to the ground on the other side of the alley. That finally gave Longarm a clear shot at the second kidnapper.

He wanted to wound the man so that he could ask him some questions—like why he and his partner were trying to grab Glorieta. But just as Longarm squeezed off a carefully aimed shot at the man's shoulder, the hombre weaved to the side, turning to run away. The bullet hit him in the throat, knocking him off his feet. Blood sprayed in the air as he dropped to the ground, looking like crimson rain as it fell through the light that came from the open door.

"Dadgum it," Longarm said. He knew he had just killed the second kidnapper. But maybe the first man was still alive.

The crowd inside the saloon had slowed itself down as everyone tried to reach the backstage area at once. Finally, several men burst out through the open door as Longarm was climbing to his feet. He supposed it really hadn't been that long; it only felt that way because sometimes the seconds seemed to tick by much more slowly during a gunfight. In reality, Longarm knew, the corpse-and-cartridge session with the two kidnappers had lasted less than a minute. Only two or three minutes had passed since Glorieta McCall started screaming.

Longarm kept his gun out as he approached the first man he'd shot. He wasn't taking any chances. However, as Jerome Horton helped Glorieta to her feet and clutched her to him, Campanella and the broken-nosed bouncer both hurried along the alley toward Longarm. Campanella held a pistol in his hand and Broken Nose was carrying a sawed-off shotgun. Both of them leveled their weapons at Longarm. "Hold it, cowboy!" Campanella cried. "Drop that gun!"

"Take it easy, old son," Longarm said. "We're on the same side." He still didn't want to reveal that he was a lawman, but he would if he had to. He toed the body that was sprawled on its back and saw the way the man's head lolled limply on his neck. The fella was dead, all right. Longarm holstered his Colt.

"I don't like having my orders ignored," Campanella said. "I told you to drop that gun, not holster it."

"And I said we're on the same side," Longarm snapped. "Ask Miss McCall. She'll tell you that I'm the one who came along and blasted those gents who were trying to drag her away from here."

Campanella turned to look at Glorieta, who was still being comforted by Horton. "Is that true, Miss McCall?"

Glorieta had her face pressed against the front of Horton's coat. She lifted her head, looked at Longarm, and nodded. Tears of fright had left streaks on her face, but even so, she was still beautiful. "That's right," she said. "This gentleman showed up just in time to save me."

Keeping his left arm around her shoulders, Horton came forward and extended his right hand to Longarm. "Thank you, sir," he said. "I'm mighty grateful that you happened along when you did."

"I didn't just happen along," Longarm said as he shook hands with Horton. "I was in the saloon listening to the lady sing. When I heard her yell after she'd gone backstage, I figured if somebody was trying to take her out of there, they'd come this way, so I circled around as fast as I could."

Horton nodded. "That was quick thinking, mister . . . ?"

"Just call me Custis."

Campanella had put up his pistol, but Broken Nose still held the scattergun. However, it was pointed toward the floor of the alley now. The saloonkeeper said to Longarm, "Yes, that was good work. I'm sorry Carl and I threatened you."

Carl had to be Broken Nose. "That's all right," Longarm said with a shrug. "You didn't know exactly what was goin' on. Reckon I'd have done the same thing if I'd been in your boots."

There was quite a crowd in the alley by now, including the young Mexican grandee and one of his bodyguards. There was still no sign of the second vaquero. The youngster was staring at Glorieta with an expression of open admiration and devotion on his face. Horton gave him a quick scowl and steered Glorieta toward the door. "Come along, my dear," he said. "Let's get you back to your dressing room so that you can rest and recover from this ordeal."

Some of the other men crowded around Longarm to slap him on the back and offer their congratulations for ventilating the would-be kidnappers. The press of well-wishers parted as a high-pitched voice called, "All right, step aside, step aside. The law's here now. Step aside."

Longarm turned to see a tall, bulky man in a high-crowned hat making his way through the crowd. He had a sheriff's star pinned to his vest. "I heard the shootin'," the man went on in his rather childlike voice. "What happened here?"

Several men spoke at once, trying to answer. The sheriff held up his hands to bring a stop to the babble.

"You there, mister," he said as he looked at Longarm. "You tell it."

Longarm did so, describing his part in the shooting but refusing to make more of it than it had been, either. When he was finished, the sheriff nodded.

"Sounds like an open-and-shut case o' self-defense," the local lawman declared. "We'll have to have an inquest and get an official verdict from the coroner's jury, though. Now, does anybody know who these here kidnappin' skunks are?"

Longarm was wondering about that himself. Both bodies were dragged into the light and laid out so the onlookers could gather around and study their faces. Longarm didn't recall ever seeing either of them before, but he knew their type: hard-featured, unshaven hombres with eyes permanently narrowed from squinting into the sun and wind. They wore range clothes that had seen better days. The only things well kept about them were their guns. Longarm had no doubt they were owlhoots.

No one in the crowd knew them, or at least no one would admit to knowing them. A couple of townies said that the dead men looked a little familiar, as if they had been around Casa Grande before, but that was all. The portly sheriff knelt beside the bodies, grunting with effort as he did so, and searched their pockets, not turning up anything except some spare cartridges for their guns and a few Mexican pesos. Here in southern Arizona Territory, there was nothing unusual about men carrying money from across the border.

"Well, some of you boys pick 'em up and tote 'em down to the undertaker's," the sheriff said as he straightened awkwardly from his crouch. "Reckon we'll never know for sure why they tried to grab that gal. Maybe they figured to hold her for ransom, or maybe they just wanted her for themselves. Either way, all they got was to wind up dead as hell." He brushed his hands together and started out of the alley. Most of the crowd followed him, including the men who picked up the two corpses.

Longarm stayed behind, though, and so did the young Mexican and his bodyguard. The youngster stepped toward Longarm and said, "Senor, I owe you the debt of gratitude."

Longarm frowned. "How do you figure that?"

"The whole world owes you this debt, for saving the beautiful and talented Señorita McCall." The man held out his hand. "I am Don Rafael Jesus y Maria Obregon Escobar Aragones."

Longarm shook hands with him. "Pleased to meet you, senor."

"Please, come inside with me. I would buy you a drink."

"No offense, but I reckon I'll pass." Longarm gestured at the smelly stains on the front of his jacket and shirt. "I'd best go back to the hotel where I'm stayin' and see if I can get these clothes sent out to a Chinese laundry."

"If you would allow me, I can see to it," Don Rafael Aragones offered. "I am staying at the best hotel in town, of course."

"No, thanks, I can handle it."

Aragones frowned darkly. "I am beginning to wonder if I should be offended by your continued refusals to accept my gratitude, senor."

"I got no problem accepting your gratitude; I just don't need any favors along with it."

Aragones looked like he still hadn't made up his mind whether to be offended or not, but he waved a slender hand and said, "Very well. *Vaya con Dios, amigo.* Perhaps we will meet again."

"Maybe," Longarm said. He had a feeling that he and Aragones probably *would* meet again.

For one thing, Longarm remembered how the youngster had said something to one of his bodyguards, after which the vaquero had disappeared and still hadn't shown up again. For another, he had seen the way Aragones looked at Glorieta McCall. Aragones had fallen hard for her. He struck Longarm as the sort of wealthy young man who was accustomed to getting whatever he wanted, whenever he wanted it. Could he have sent that vaquero outside to see about setting up an attempt to grab the girl when the show was over?

That was just a hunch, and Longarm had no way of knowing if there was any truth to the idea. But until he knew for sure, he wasn't ready to rule it out, either.

Of course, he told himself as he left the alley and headed toward his hotel, none of it had anything to do with the job that had brought him here, other than the connection with Jerome Horton. But Longarm had learned over the years to keep an open mind about everything involved with an investigation. Sometimes there were more twists and turns in a case than a sidewinding rattler leaves in a dirt trail.

And as with a sidewinder, sometimes a fella just didn't know when or where trouble was going to strike. All he could do was hope he heard the warning rattle in time. . . .

The local undertaker was also the coroner. He convened the inquest the next morning in the town hall. The jury heard testimony from Longarm, Glorieta McCall, and Sheriff Andy Finch, after which they wasted no time in returning a verdict. According to the jury, the two deceased, still unidentified, had met their maker in a case of self-defense at the hands of one Custis Parker. Longarm didn't much cotton to the idea of giving a phony name in an official proceeding, but he still wanted to keep his true identity to himself. And since Parker really was his middle name, it wasn't like he was stretching the truth too much.

When the inquest was over, Jerome Horton and Glorieta McCall came up to him. "Thank you again," Glorieta said as she gave him a gloved hand. She wore a dark green outfit and a hat with a small feather on it. Now that she wasn't scared out of her wits and hadn't been crying, she was lovelier than ever, Longarm thought. "I'm convinced that you saved my life, Mr. Parker."

"I don't know about that. Seems to me that if those two hombres had wanted to kill you, they could have done it backstage and not tried to haul you out of there."

"Regardless of their intent, we can be sure it didn't bode well for Miss McCall," Horton said crisply. "Do you have a few moments, Mr. Parker? There's a matter I'd like to discuss with you."

Longarm shrugged. "I don't reckon there's anywhere I have to be."

"Excellent. I'll escort Miss McCall back to the hotel, then meet you in the office at my business down the street. It's the Southwestern Freighting and Express Company."

"I think I remember seeing the place when I rode in yesterday," Longarm said. "I'll mosey on down there."

"I'll be there in a few minutes," Horton promised. He linked arms with Glorieta. "Come along, my dear."

The inquest had been well attended, but the crowd was dispersing rapidly now that it was over. Longarm had looked for Rafael Aragones but hadn't seen any sign of the young Mexican.

As he started down the street toward the freight company barn, Sheriff Andy Finch came up and fell in step alongside him. "You're a mighty handy man with a gun, ain't you, Parker?" Finch asked.

"What makes you say that?"

"Those two gents you killed looked like they were mighty well acquainted with which end of the barrel the bullet comes out of. But you didn't seem to have no trouble with them."

"I wouldn't say that. A couple of those slugs came close enough to almost part my hair for me."

"Maybe. I'm just wonderin' what you're doin' here in Casa Grande."

"Passin' through," Longarm said.

"On your way to where, from where?"

Longarm's eyes narrowed. "You know, most of the time questions like that ain't considered polite west of the Mississippi."

"Not when it's a lawman askin' them," Finch insisted. "Polite ain't got nothin' to do with it."

"Well, Sheriff, in that case . . . I've been cowboyin' over Texas way for a spell, but I'm tired of it. Thought I'd head for California and see what it's like out there."

"Is that so? You wouldn't have the name of the spread you been ridin' for in Texas, happen I should want to check up on your story, would you?"

"As a matter of fact," Longarm said, "you can get in touch with Miss Jessica Starbuck at the Circle Star Ranch and ask her, if you want." The Circle Star was the largest ranch in West Texas, and its owner, Jessie Starbuck, was

23

one of Longarm's best friends in the world. If anyone asked, she would have nothing but good things to say about "Custis Parker."

Finch rubbed his chin. Obviously, he had heard of Jessie and her ranching empire. "The Circle Star, eh? Well, I reckon I can take your word for it. I just don't want no gunslinger trouble around here."

"From what I've heard, you've already got trouble in these parts."

"What do you mean by that?" Finch asked quickly.

"Outlaws have been raiding the gold and silver shipments from the mines in the area, haven't they?"

"Not in my jurisdiction, they ain't!" Finch followed that exclamation with a shrug. "But yeah, some of the shipments have been hit. I reckon those bandits know to stay away from Casa Grande, though."

Longarm didn't make any reply to that, but he doubted if the outlaws were scared of Sheriff Finch. They just hadn't gotten around to striking in the Casa Grande area yet.

Not wanting to make the lawman too suspicious, Longarm decided to indulge his curiosity regarding another subject. "You know a young Mexican named Aragones? Dresses fancy, probably has plenty of *dinero*."

"Don Rafael? Oh, yeah, I know him." Finch didn't sound too pleased by that, either. "His pa is Don Hernando Aragones, who owns one of the biggest spreads in Sonora. The old don ain't a bad fella, but young Rafe . . . well, he can be a ring-tailed terror when he wants to be. Spoiled rotten and thinks the rest of the world is here just to hand over whatever he wants."

Longarm nodded. "He struck me the same way. Has he been in any real trouble around here?"

"No, not really. Got a little rough with a few whores, but they shut up complainin' pretty quick when he offered to pay them extra. He's been in some worse scrapes down

24

in Tucson, but the old don's got enough money and influence to get the boy out of the woodshed pretty quick." Finch slanted a look at Longarm. "Why're you so interested in Rafe Aragones?"

"Just curious," Longarm said with a shake of his head. "I talked to him a little last night, after the dust-up in the alley beside the Golden Horde. Didn't like him much."

The sheriff grunted. "You an' me both."

They had reached the express company barn. "I'm supposed to talk to Mr. Horton," Longarm said. "Maybe I'll see you later, Sheriff."

"Horton's probably gonna offer you a reward for savin' that gal last night. If I was you, Parker, I'd take it. Money like that would go a long way toward gettin' you to California."

Longarm grinned at the lawman. "Is that your way of tellin' me you'll be glad to see me leave town, Sheriff?"

"I don't like gunplay in Casa Grande," Finch said. "Not even when it's in a good cause."

He left Longarm there. Longarm watched the sheriff amble off down the street like a bear looking for berries. Then he went inside the office and found the old man called Salty sitting behind a desk, hat tilted down over his eyes, feet propped on the desk. Heavy snores made the white beard flutter a little.

Longarm thought about yelling "Apaches!" and seeing how high the old man would jump. That would be a downright mean thing to do, though, so he just grinned and said, "Wake up, Salty."

"Huh? What?" Salty sat up so fast that his chair nearly fell over. His feet thudded to the floor and he caught his balance. He glared up at Longarm. "What the hell's the idea, comin' in here and disturbin' a fella while he's workin'?"

"The only work you were doin', old-timer, is sawin' wood."

25

"You oughta be more respectful o' your elders, boy. You'll be old yourself one o' these days."

"Sooner rather than later," Longarm said. "Anyway, Horton's on his way down here, and I didn't figure you'd want the boss to catch you sleeping."

"Huh! If he don't like what I'm doin', he can danged well fire me! I ain't never been buffaloed, not by no-body—" Salty stopped short, shot to his feet, and snatched his hat off as the door opened and Jerome Horton came into the office. "Howdy there, Mr. Horton. What can I do for you?"

"I just want to borrow the office for a few minutes to talk to Mr. Parker here," Horton explained.

"You don't have to borrow nothin', sir; the whole place is yours, after all. I'll just go out in the barn and give you gents some privacy." The old-timer hustled out through the door that led into the main part of the barn.

Horton went behind the desk and motioned for Longarm to have a seat in the room's other chair. Longarm turned it around and straddled it, then took a cheroot from his shirt pocket, and put it unlit in his mouth. "That old-timer's quite a character," he commented.

"Salty?" Horton asked as he sat down in the chair behind the desk. "Yes, he is. A good man, though. He's been with the company for quite a while, and he's been knocking around these parts for even longer. He doesn't drive as much for me as he used to, but he's done a good job running the office here. I'm going to have to replace him, though."

Longarm frowned. "You're not fixing to fire him, are you? It ain't none of my business, but he's such a likable old cuss . . ."

"Fire him? Not at all." Horton waved off the very idea. "I have another, more important job for him, and it's related to the reason that I asked you to come down here, Mr. Parker."

26

Longarm's frowned deepened. "I reckon I don't understand."

Horton leaned forward and clasped his hands together on the desk. "I mean that I have a job for you, too, Mr. Parker. I want you—and to be blunt, I want your gun—to come to work for me."

Chapter 3

Longarm hadn't been expecting that. He shifted the unlit cheroot from one side of his mouth to the other and narrowed his eyes as he looked across the desk at Horton. After a moment, he said, "You may have the wrong idea about me, mister."

Horton held up both hands. "I meant no offense, Mr. Parker. All I meant was that you seem to be very handy with your gun, and I have need of someone to watch out for Miss McCall."

"Like a bodyguard, you mean?"

"Exactly! If it hadn't been for you, God knows what might have happened last night when those men attacked Glorieta."

"Both of those gents are dead," Longarm pointed out. "I don't reckon they'll be bothering her again."

"Not those two, of course. But I believe that she's still in danger. Have you heard of a man named Don Rafael Aragones?"

Longarm didn't see any point in denying it. "I've even met the fella. Sort of an arrogant young rascal."

"He's worse than that," Horton said. "He's a dangerous man. I don't think he'd stop at murder to get what he wants. And if you saw the way he was looking at Miss McCall last night, you know that he wants *her*."

From the sound of it, Horton had formed a theory similar to the one that had come to Longarm. "You think this Aragones had something to do with those varmints who tried to kidnap Miss McCall?"

"I'm almost certain of it," Horton said. His hands clenched into fists, and his eyes glittered with the anger he felt toward Aragones.

"Those two hombres I had to ventilate were gringos, not Mexicans," Longarm said. "And nobody knew who they were, including Aragones."

Horton snorted. "You don't expect him to admit that they worked for him, do you? Quite a few men from his father's ranch travel with him when he comes across the border, and Don Hernando has American cowboys riding for him as well as vaqueros. Rough men, little better than outlaws. It's entirely possible those two came from the camp Aragones has just outside of town."

What Horton was saying made sense. Longarm had come up with pretty much the same idea himself. "Maybe you're right," he admitted. "If Aragones was behind what happened, do you think he'll try again, considerin' what happened to those fellas?"

"I think being denied what he wants will make him more determined than ever to have it. That's why I want you to go along on the tour."

"Tour?" Longarm repeated. "What tour?"

"Glorieta and I have decided to travel through southern Arizona so that she can perform in some of the other towns before she makes her grand debut in Tucson." Horton smiled, obviously enjoying his role as promoter of Glorieta McCall's singing career. "I've already sent telegrams to people I know in Gila Bend, Yuma, Ehrenberg, and Hardyville, arranging appearances for her."

Longarm recognized the names of all the settlements

Horton had mentioned. His job had taken him to all of them at one time or another in the past. "You're going up the Colorado River," he said. It wasn't a question.

"Yes, by riverboat from Yuma to Hardyville," Horton said. "I have business in all those places, so I'll be able to kill two birds with one stone."

Longarm was willing to bet that the "business" Horton was talking about had something to do with picking up gold and silver shipments. The precious minerals flowed into Gila Bend and Yuma from mines to the south and into Ehrenberg and Hardyville from diggings on both sides of the Colorado River. If the bullion-raiding gang was working its way across Arizona, as seemed likely, the outlaws were heading toward some very rich pickings indeed.

The wheels of Longarm's brain clicked over rapidly. Working for Horton would give him a perfect excuse for being on hand if there were any more robberies. Not only that, but he felt an instinctive dislike for Rafael Aragones, and if the young grandee was responsible for the kidnapping attempt on Glorieta McCall, she probably really did need some protection. Two birds with one stone, Horton had said. Longarm found himself in agreement.

"Well, Mr. Parker, what do you say?" Horton prodded.

Longarm stood up and stuck out his paw. "You got yourself a deal, Mr. Horton. When do I start?"

"Right away," Horton said as he shook hands with Longarm. "We're going to be here in Casa Grande one more night, so that Glorieta can sing at the Golden Horde again."

"I thought that was a one night only deal."

"Originally it was, but Vincente Campanella was so pleased with the way the performance went—until the trouble afterward, of course—that he asked if Glorieta would mind doing another show tonight. I left it up to her, and she agreed."

"So we'll be leaving for Gila Bend tomorrow?"

"That's right. I have a special coach that Miss McCall and I use, and all our luggage is carried in another wagon. I'm recruiting Salty to drive the coach, since it's going to be a longer trip than I intended when we left Tucson, and he's the best jehu in this part of the country."

Longarm was pleased that Salty would be traveling with them. The colorful old man would keep things interesting, at least.

"Now, I want you to move into the Ames House," Horton went on. "That's the hotel where Miss McCall and I are staying. I'll want you to be close to her at all times, in case of trouble."

Longarm nodded. "I understand."

"You haven't asked about your wages."

"I figure you'll pay whatever is fair," Longarm said. "I can tell Miss McCall means a lot to you."

"She's like the daughter I never had," Horton said. "I couldn't bear it if anything happened to her."

"I'll look out for her," Longarm promised. He didn't figure Horton really meant that about Glorieta being like a daughter to him, but that was none of his business. His job was just to keep her safe if Aragones, or anybody else, threatened her. And to catch the outlaws who'd been holding up those bullion shipments, of course. Any way you looked at it, he had a pretty full plate.

But there was only one way to eat it—just like the apple—one bite at a time.

Longarm's saddle was at the livery stable where he'd put up the buckskin the night before. He got his warbag and Winchester from the hotel where he'd been staying and moved them to the Ames House, where the clerk at the desk was expecting him. "Yes, sir, Mr. Horton told me you'd be coming along," the man said. "If you'll just follow me, I'll take you upstairs. You'll have the room directly across from the suite where Mr. Horton and Miss McCall are staying."

The bed in the room was a big four-poster with a mattress that was too soft. Gauzy curtains hung over the windows and the rug on the floor was thick. A mahogany chifforobe on one side of the room was polished to a high shine. Longarm knew he was going to feel a bit out of place here, but he supposed he could stand it for one night. He was just going to have to get used to the lap of luxury, he told himself with a grin.

He had just finished settling in—leaning the rifle in one corner, hanging his hat on a bedpost, and tossing his warbag on the bed—when a soft knock sounded on the door. He wasn't expecting trouble, but as he went to the door, he rested his hand on the butt of his Colt. "Who is it?" he asked through the panel.

"Glorieta McCall."

Her speaking voice had the same throaty quality that it did when she sang. Longarm opened the door. Glorieta stood there with a smile on her face, her red hair loose now and tumbling in waves around her shoulders. She wore a dark blue gown rather than the green outfit she'd had on earlier.

"Hello, Mr. Parker," she said. "I assume the fact that you're here means you've accepted Jerome's offer of employment."

She talked a mite fancy for a gal who'd been slinging hash in a Chinaman's place not that long ago, Longarm thought, but he said, "That's right. He thinks you still may be in danger, and I reckon I agree with him."

"Everyone who's alive is in some sort of danger, aren't they?"

"Well, I suppose you could look at it that way. In your case, it's a little more specific, though."

"I know. Rafael Aragones."

"You agree with the way Mr. Horton feels about him?"

"I think Rafael Aragones is a dangerous man. No more so than you, though, Mr. Parker." She smiled again. "Could I come in? I don't like standing in the hall."

Longarm stepped back. "Sure, come on in." He made no move to close the door behind her.

Glorieta noticed. "Close the door, please," she said.

Longarm didn't move. He didn't like being ordered around. Glorieta McCall was undeniably beautiful, but she was starting to rub him the wrong way.

"I'm sorry," she said abruptly. "I sound like a real bitch, don't I? I guess that comes from being dirt poor most of my life and then suddenly having money when I thought I never would."

Longarm liked her better now. He closed the door and gestured toward an overstuffed armchair in one corner of the room. "Have a seat." She had been around Horton for a while; maybe he could find out something from her about the bullion robberies. Chances were, Horton told her things that he might not tell anyone else.

He didn't want to rush into that, though. Too many questions might make her suspicious of his real reason for being here.

She sat down, and as she did, the skirt of her gown parted a little and allowed him a look at her stocking-clad calves. They were as nicely turned as he expected them to be. She didn't seem to be in a hurry to cover them up, either, and when she finally did, he thought he saw a flirtatious glint in her green eyes.

"Where are you from, Mr. Parker?" she asked.

"Call me Custis."

"Only if you call me Glorieta."

"Deal," Longarm said with a grin. "I hail from West-by-God Virginia. Came out here after the Billy Yanks and Johnny Rebs decided to stop shootin' at each other, and I've been one place or another ever since."

"You don't look old enough to have been in the war."

"I was in it, all right. Just don't ask me on which side, because I disremember."

Glorieta laughed. "I understand. It doesn't really matter now, does it?"

"Not as far as I can see. And my eyes are pretty good." Longarm perched a hip on the footboard of the bed. "How about you? I've heard that you grew up out here in these parts."

A change came over her face then. Not a hardening, exactly, but a sense that some sort of barrier had dropped. "I don't like to talk about that," she said.

"Fair enough. Consider the subject dropped." To prove it, he went on, "I surely did enjoy your singing last night. Don't tell the boss, but I almost would've taken the job of looking out for you just so I could hear you sing some more."

"Thank you. I really don't know if I'm any good at it or not. I've just always enjoyed singing."

"You're good," Longarm assured her. "Better than most I've heard."

"Now you're just flattering me," Glorieta said with a smile.

Longarm raised his right hand. "Nope, you got my word of honor on it. I can see why Mr. Horton thought you ought to be singin' in theaters and opera houses."

"Well . . . maybe someday. Right now, I think saloons are better. That way, the audiences will have had enough who-hit-John so that they won't care how I sing."

Longarm laughed. That was Glorieta's true nature coming out, he thought. She might put on airs sometimes, but she was still a Western gal at heart. "I think they'll enjoy the shows, no matter how much they drink."

"I hope so." She came to her feet. "I really should be going." She moved closer to him and laid a hand on his arm. "You'll be close by in case I need you, won't you?"

Now there was no mistaking the look in her eyes. Long-

35

arm didn't know the exact nature of the relationship between her and Horton, but he could tell what she had in mind for him. And he wasn't sure if he liked the idea or not. While Glorieta McCall was a beautiful young woman, and he naturally felt himself drawn to her, it might complicate things too much if he wound up in bed with her.

Quietly, he said, "I ain't sure the boss would like it much if I stayed *too* close to you."

"Don't worry about Jerome," she said as she looked up into his eyes. "He's a precious old dear, but that's all." She moved her hand from Longarm's arm to his cheek. "I'm very grateful to you for helping me last night, Mr. Parker . . . Custis. I like to express my gratitude."

With that, she lifted her face to his and kissed him, coming up on her toes in order to do so. His arms instinctively went around her, pulling her against him. He was being a damned fool and he knew it. All Glorieta had to do was run to Horton and tell him what had happened, and Longarm would find himself out of a job. It didn't really matter, of course; he was here on Uncle Sam's business, not Horton's. But since the situation had worked out so that he had a ready-made excuse for sticking close to the freight company owner, he didn't want to ruin it first thing.

Logically, he knew that. But with his arms full of a soft, warm, passionate woman—who obviously wasn't wearing a whole hell of a lot under that gown—logic didn't mean much. Glorieta's full, firm breasts were mashed against his chest, and her lips parted so that her tongue could dart against his mouth. He met those thrusts with his own tongue. He was erect by now, his manhood prodding against the softness of her belly. She pushed her hips against him so that the contact was even more arousing.

When she finally drew back, breaking the kiss, they were both breathing harder than they had been before.

"We won't say anything about this to Jerome," she said.

"Nope, I reckon not," Longarm agreed.

"Later, when the time is right . . ." She left the rest unsaid, but Longarm knew what she meant. He nodded. He wanted Glorieta McCall. Maybe it wasn't right, but, Lord, he wanted her, like a man lost in the desert wants a cold, clear spring.

She slipped out of his arms and put her hand on the doorknob, then looked back at him. "You'll stay close, in case of trouble?" she asked again.

He nodded. Him staying close to her was one thing she didn't have to worry about.

The Golden Horde Saloon was just as crowded for Glorieta's second performance as it had been the night before. As Longarm looked around the room, he saw many of the same faces. Quite a few members of the audience had come back to hear Glorieta sing again.

Not surprisingly, Don Rafael Aragones was sitting at one of the tables down front, accompanied by the two vaqueros. The second one had finally shown up again. If Aragones had been behind the kidnapping attempt the night before, would he be foolish enough—or obsessed enough with Glorieta—to try something again tonight? Longarm hoped that wouldn't be the case. He wanted to be able to concentrate on his real job and not have to spend too much time guarding the Arizona Flame.

Tonight he stood off to one side rather than at the bar, close enough to the stage that he could get there in a couple of bounds if need be. Broken Nose Carl was on the other side of the stage, equally vigilant. Vincente Campanella sat at a front table with Horton, their clash of the day—over money and ticket sales—forgotten now. Both men were getting what they wanted: Campanella, a lucrative attraction for his saloon, and Horton, plenty of exposure for Glorieta and a good start for her career.

She came out and sang, mostly the same songs she had performed the night before with a few different ones thrown in for good measure, and the crowd went wild, just as Longarm expected. In a rough frontier town like Casa Grande, the male population hardly ever saw a female as lovely as Glorieta McCall, let alone one who had some actual talent.

It was a foregone conclusion that Glorieta would do an encore. She retreated behind the curtain, but from where Longarm was positioned, he could see her standing in the wings, waiting for the applause and cheers to build to a suitable level before she came out again. That was planned; he had suggested before the show that she stay where he could keep an eye on her, even though she would be out of the audience's view. She looked over at him and lifted a hand. Longarm thought she was going to wave at him, but instead she brought her hand to one of her breasts and squeezed it, then moved her hand to the other breast and caressed it. She gave him a sensuous smile.

One thing you could say for her, Longarm thought: the gal sure wasn't shy. She was downright brazen about what she wanted. Longarm was beginning to believe that Glorieta really wasn't sleeping with Jerome Horton. Otherwise, she wouldn't be acting like she was toward her new bodyguard.

Longarm just smiled faintly at her. Out here in full view of the audience, there was nothing else he could do. Glorieta blew him a kiss, and then she was all business again. She was ready to go out and do that encore.

Glorieta had just stepped out on stage when Longarm heard a popping sound that was barely audible over the uproar inside the saloon. It took him a moment to realize what he was hearing was gunfire. Right about then, somebody yelled near the entrance. More men took up the shout, until a sudden alarmed silence fell. Longarm was already making his way toward the front of the saloon. He shouldered men out of the way as he went to see what the trouble was. A glance back told him that Glorieta was still standing there on stage, looking as confused as everyone else in the saloon seemed to be. The thought crossed Longarm's mind that the shots could have been a distraction set up by Rafael Aragones so that his men could try again to snatch the Arizona Flame. They'd have a hard time doing it with her standing in full view of the entire audience, though.

He saw quickly that the commotion had nothing to do with Aragones. The old-timer called Salty was inside the batwings, holding up the bloodstained figure of another man. "Mr. Horton! Mr. Horton!" Salty shouted over the tumult. "The shipment's been hit! Mr. Horton!"

Longarm felt his pulse speed up. Horton hadn't said anything to him about expecting a bullion shipment. Of course, there wouldn't have been any reason for the freight company owner to mention that to a man he had hired as a bodyguard for his musical protégée.

Longarm checked again and saw that Broken Nose Carl was staying close to the stage and Glorieta. Satisfied that she was safe for the moment, he bulled on through the crowd and came up to help Salty with the injured man. "What happened?" Longarm asked as they steered the man toward a table. "What were those shots outside?"

"That was me, tryin' to get folks' attention," Salty admitted as they lowered the injured man into a chair. "When Wilt come in all shot up, I knew I had to get help in a hurry. This seemed the most likely place."

Longarm couldn't find any fault with that reasoning. Most of the people in Casa Grande who were still awake were in the Golden Horde Saloon, including, Longarm saw a moment later, the town doctor. The crowd parted to let the portly, white-haired man through. He set a black medical bag on the table and ordered, "Get that shirt off him so I can see how bad he's hit."

Salty did as he was told, ripping the wounded man's shirt and revealing an ugly-looking bullet hole in his side. The man had bled quite a bit, but to Longarm's experienced eye, it looked as if he might have a good chance to pull through, providing that the slug hadn't done too much damage inside him. The doctor set to work cleaning the wound.

Jerome Horton reached the table, having taken longer to get there because he had been all the way at the front of the room. So had Longarm, but Horton lacked his bulk and ability to push through a crowd. Horton's face was pale and drawn as he took hold of Salty's arm and asked, "What the hell happened?"

Longarm listened intently as the old man explained. "Wilt come into town a few minutes ago on one o' the pack mules. He was by hisself and all shot up, so I knowed there had been trouble. I come down here right away to get help."

"But where are the rest of the men? And the other mules and their cargo?"

"The men are all dead," Salty said, his voice grim. "Wilt was able to tell me that much, even though he was mostly out of his head from losin' so much blood. The mules are all gone, along with the bullion."

Horton swayed a little, as if he were fighting not to pass out. "All gone," he muttered, and Longarm thought he was talking about the stolen bullion. His opinion of the man went up some as Horton added, "Those poor men."

"Wilt said they never had a chance." Salty's voice shook with anger now. "They was bushwhacked just as they come up out of a little canyon. No warnin', no chance to surrender, just a whole damned volley outta the night, cuttin' 'em down."

40

Longarm felt angry himself when he heard that. The gang of bullion thieves he was after had always been trigger-happy, but this was the first time they had carried out such a massacre. Whoever was leading them must have decided it would be easier just to go ahead and kill all the men with the mule train.

"Reckon Wilt passed out when he was hit, and those damned owlhoots took him for dead," Salty went on. "He's lucky none of 'em put another slug in him just to make sure. When he come to, the rest of the men were dead, and the mules were all gone except for one he found wanderin' around not far off. And the packsaddle it had been carryin' was gone. The outlaws must've tried to shift the load or somethin', and the mule took off for the tall and uncut once the saddle was off of it. That was more luck for Wilt, the poor ol' son of a bitch."

The fondness in Salty's tone told Longarm that the old-timer was fond of the wounded man. Probably they had worked together for quite a while.

Wearily, Horton scrubbed a hand over his face. He turned to the doctor and asked, "How is he? Will he be all right?"

"I hope so." The doctor finished tying a makeshift bandage around the wounded man's torso. "I want to get him to my office so I can make a more complete examination. Some of you boys grab hold and pick him up. Gentle, now!"

The wounded man was lifted and carried out of the saloon. The doctor and several other men followed. As soon as they had gone out, Sheriff Finch came in. The local lawman looked shaken.

"I just heard what happened, Mr. Horton," Finch said. "Was it the same bunch that hit your other shipments?"

"I'm sure it was," Horton said. "They have to be stopped, Sheriff. This time they've murdered close to a dozen of my men."

41

Finch swallowed hard. "I'll gather up a posse and see what I can do. It ain't easy trackin' at night, though."

Horton nodded absently. He looked around, and his gaze fell on Longarm. Horton stepped over to him.

"You heard?" Horton asked.

Longarm nodded. "I sure did. Sounds mighty bad."

"Mr. Parker, do you think you could go along with Sheriff Finch and the posse?"

Before Longarm could answer, Salty declared, "I'll damn sure go! Wilt is a pard of mine from way back!"

Longarm wanted to go with the posse, of course, since his real job was to track down the gang of robbers. But Horton had hired him to look out for Glorieta, and Longarm wanted to maintain that pose in case things didn't work out tonight.

"I reckon I could," he said after a second's hesitation, "if you're sure Miss McCall will be all right."

He and Horton both looked at the stage, where Glorieta still stood, looking worried and tense. Horton said, "I'll stick close to her tonight, and I'm sure I can persuade Campanella to let me post Carl in the hall right outside our suite. Please, Mr. Parker. Glorieta means the world to me, as you know, but this is important, too."

Murder always was, Longarm thought. He nodded and looked over at Finch. "You've got another member for your posse, Sheriff. I'll be ready to ride whenever you are."

Chapter 4

The posse was ready to pull out of Casa Grande less than fifteen minutes later. In addition to Longarm, Salty, and Sheriff Finch, the group included more than twenty cowboys, miners, and townsmen, all of whom had been in the Golden Horde listening to Glorieta McCall sing. Longarm had saddled the buckskin, then gone up to his room in the Ames House to fetch his Winchester. Salty was well armed, too, carrying a Sharps buffalo gun and packing a long-barreled Remington on his hip. The rest of the posse bristled with rifles and shotguns, some of them personal weapons, others handed out by the sheriff. No one wanted to go up against as vicious a bunch as the bullion robbers without packing plenty of firepower.

Longarm could tell that Sheriff Finch was nervous. The lawman wasn't a coward; otherwise he would not have been able to maintain order in a town like Casa Grande, which still had plenty of rough edges to it. But he had probably never come up against a bunch of owlhoots like this before, either. These bandits struck without warning and killed without mercy.

"We'd better keep our eyes peeled," Longarm commented to the sheriff as the posse rode south from Casa

Grande into rough, semidesert country. "Hombres like these are liable to leave a few men behind to watch their back trail and bushwhack anybody who tries to follow them."

Finch grunted. "You sound like you know how an outlaw's mind works, fella." His tone was suspicious.

Longarm suppressed the irritation he felt. "That's just common sense, Sheriff," he said.

"Sounds pretty dang sensible to me," Salty put in. He was riding in the forefront of the posse along with Longarm and Finch. The old-timer knew exactly where the massacre had taken place, because he was more familiar with the trails used by the mule trains than anyone else in these parts.

"Yeah, I reckon you're right," Finch agreed reluctantly. His head moved constantly, swiveling from right to left on his thick neck as he watched for any signs of an ambush.

The moon had started to lower in the sky by the time they reached the spot where the mule train had been ambushed. The silvery orb still cast enough illumination so that Longarm could see the dark shapes sprawled on the sandy ground. His jaw tightened in anger as he reined in along with the others.

"They were waitin' in the brush on both sides o' the trail," Salty said, pointing to where the outlaws had been concealed. About fifty yards ahead, the trail dipped into a shallow canyon. "Down below the bluffs, Wilt and the rest o' the boys couldn't see nothin', so they didn't expect no trouble. Soon as they was all out in the open, the sons o' bitches cut loose at 'em." Salty shook his head. "They never had a chance. Not a chance in hell."

Longarm, Sheriff Finch, and several of the possemen dismounted to check the bodies. Wilt had been right—they were all dead. The mule drovers had been a mixed group, some American but mostly Mexican. In a quiet voice, Longarm asked Salty, "What mine was this train coming from?"

"There are three down south of here: the Jackpot, the Seven Burros, and the Cat's Claw. They all use the stamp mill at the Jackpot and ship their bullion from there."

"So this was a good-sized shipment?"

Salty nodded. "Yep. Prob'ly between twenty an' thirty thousand dollars worth o' gold and silver." He looked at the bodies of the slain drovers. "But not even that's worth the lives o' these men."

"No," Longarm agreed, "it's sure as hell not."

"The undertaker's wagon is on the way from town," Sheriff Finch said. "Ought to be here by sunup, so these bodies can be got back in before the hottest part of the day. I'll leave one man here to keep the coyotes and buzzards off of them, and the rest of us will push on. Salty, did Wilt have any idea which way them varmints went?"

The old-timer shook his grizzled head. "No, they was all gone by the time he came to, and he didn't take the time to look for a trail. He wanted to get to town 'fore he passed out again."

"Well, we'll have to scout around then," Finch said. "Who's got the best eyes?"

Longarm figured there was a good chance he had followed more trails than everybody else in the posse put together, not counting an old-timer like Salty. Leading his horse, he walked in a big circle around the ambush site, hunkering down on his heels a few times to study the ground more closely. The moonlight was fading. The best he could hope to do now was to start the posse off in the right direction.

Finally he straightened and said, "They headed west. No way of knowing how far they went in that direction before changing course, if they did."

"Nothin' much over there but a few stubby mountains and a bunch of desert," Salty commented. "Once they'd gone a ways, they prob'ly either turned north toward Gila Bend or south toward the border."

"Well, we got to go after them," Finch said. "We can't let 'em get away with this."

"I wouldn't go more than a mile or two before morning," Longarm advised. "That way if we've lost the trail in the darkness, we won't have to backtrack so far to pick it up again once the sun's up."

Finch rubbed his beard-stubbled jaw for a moment, then nodded. He probably didn't like taking Longarm's advice, but it made sense. "We'll go a mile or two west, then wait until it's light. Shouldn't be more'n a couple of hours."

The posse members mounted up and got ready to ride west. The one man who was left behind to guard the bodies pushed his hat to the back of his head and said, "I sure wish I was goin' with you boys. Hangin' around with a bunch of dead folks makes me a mite leery."

"They can't hurt you," Longarm told him. "It's the live ones you got to worry about."

The posse was lucky. Longarm and Salty were able to find the trail of the outlaws without much trouble, even before the sun came up, as soon as the sky had lightened enough for them to see fairly well. The tracks still led west. The posse was already on the move by the time the sun poked its shining face above the eastern horizon.

Longarm was tired, not having gotten any sleep the night before, but he had taken part in enough of these chases so that he knew how to reach inside himself and find reserves of strength and stamina. Salty was the same way, the sort of old buzzard who was tough as whang leather. Sheriff Andy Finch, though, had been softened by town life, and he began to look haggard as the morning wore on. So did most of the other possemen. If they didn't catch up to the outlaws before the day was over, they would start suggesting that the posse turn back. Finch would probably go along with that, citing a lack of jurisdiction. Longarm didn't know if they were out of the county yet, but they had to be getting close to the line.

If that happened, Longarm might have to reveal that he was a deputy U.S. marshal and didn't have to worry about jurisdiction as long as he didn't cross any international boundaries. He would eat that bite of the apple when he came to it, though, he told himself.

Late in the morning, as they were passing one of the scrubby mountains that dotted the mostly arid landscape, Longarm suddenly saw something flash on the slope. Instantly, he yelled, "Get down!" and flung himself out of the saddle, kicking his feet free of the stirrups as he did so. He heard the wind-rip of a bullet passing close by his head. As he landed on the ground and rolled over, another slug pulverized a fist-sized rock next to him, spraying him with dust and sharp little fragments.

One of the posse members cried out. When Longarm looked in that direction, he saw the man toppling out of the saddle, clutching a bloody, bullet-shattered shoulder. Another man grunted and doubled over, hit somewhere in the body. Bullets were flying all around the men, buzzing like angry hornets.

Salty was down off his horse, too, which would make him a more difficult target to hit. Finch was still mounted and was struggling to bring his frantically rearing horse under control. The animal must have spooked because of the smell of blood, Longarm thought. Several members of the posse were hit and bleeding badly.

Longarm surged to his feet and lunged toward his horse. His hand closed around the stock of the Winchester sticking up from the saddle sheath. He hauled out the rifle and broke into a run toward a small gully he had spotted. It was about thirty feet away, and thirty feet was a long way when a fella was being shot at. A couple of bullets kicked up dust around his feet, but he made it to the gully unhit and threw himself forward into it, landing belly down in the dirt.

The impact knocked the breath out of him for a moment. He caught it as fast as he could, because the posse was still trapped out there in the open. When he could see straight again, he thrust the barrel of the Winchester over the lip of the gully and opened fire, blasting shots toward the slope where he had seen the sun reflect off a gun barrel.

He was certain now that was what he had seen. For a split second, he'd had his doubts, thinking that maybe the reflection was something else. Now there was no doubt at all in his mind. The wounded men lying on the ground or hunched over in their saddles were all the proof anybody needed that the posse was being bushwhacked.

With a grunt, Salty landed in the gully beside Longarm, holding his Sharps. "Dad*gum* it!" the old man exclaimed. "We rode right into that one, didn't we? Reckon it would've been worse if you hadn't hollered, though. What happened? You see the sun flash on a rifle barrel?"

"That's right," Longarm confirmed as he dropped lower in the gully and started fishing cartridges out of his pockets. The Winchester was empty. As he thumbed the fresh cartridges through the rifle's loading gate, he looked up and down the gully and saw that half a dozen more men had dived into it while he was giving them covering fire. He glanced over his shoulder at the rest of the posse. The ones who could still ride were hightailing it, led by Sheriff Finch.

"That damn tub o' lard!" Salty said, looking in the same direction as Longarm. "He's runnin' off and leavin' us here!"

Longarm didn't have a very high opinion of Finch, either, but to be fair about it, the sheriff had several wounded men on his hands. Maybe he was just trying to get them to safety before joining Longarm, Salty, and the handful of other men in trying to fight off the ambushers. That wasn't likely, Longarm thought, but it was possible.

For now he couldn't waste time and energy worrying about Finch and the others. He said to Salty, "I've only spotted three or four puffs of gun smoke from up there. We outnumber the bastards."

"Yeah, but they got the high ground and all we got is this piddlin' little gully. They can keep us pinned down here as long as they want."

"We'll make it hot for them while they try," Longarm said.

Salty grinned at him. "Now you're talkin'." The old-timer patted the stock of his Sharps. "All I got to do is nick one of 'em with this buffalo gun to put him out of the fight."

Longarm knew that was true. The slugs thrown by the big Sharps packed enough punch so that even a minor wound would put a man down and keep him down. "Pick your target," he said. "Let 'em know this dog's still got teeth."

He opened fire with the Winchester again, spraying bullets across the hillside where he knew the bushwhackers were concealed. Beside him, the Sharps exploded with a heavy boom, and farther along the gully, the other members of the posse who were holed up there started firing as well.

Longarm grimaced as a return bullet struck the ground in front of the gully and threw dirt in his face. He blinked his eyes to clear them and directed his fire toward the spot where he thought the shot had come from, emptying the Winchester for the second time. Salty had reloaded and now fired again, the blast of the buffalo gun sending echoes rolling across the mostly flat terrain.

Longarm kept up his assault on the slope. After a while, he noticed that the bushwhackers' shots had slacked off. Finally, they died away to nothing. Longarm wasn't surprised a few minutes later when he saw a dust cloud rising on the other side of a rocky shoulder that jutted out from the mountain.

"They've pulled up stakes," he said as he started to thumb fresh cartridges into the Winchester yet again. "We made it too warm for them. Anyway, they did what they set out to do."

"Ruin this here posse?" Salty said.

Longarm nodded grimly. "That's right. There's only about a third of us left. The others are wounded or took off with Sheriff Finch or both."

"We can't go after that gang by ourselves," Salty said, sounding disappointed.

Longarm started to tell him that they could do just that, but he thought better of it. The two of them would have no chance against such a large, ruthless gang. Besides, there were the wounded to think of.

And the dead. Two members of the posse had succumbed to their wounds, Longarm and Salty found when they checked the injured men a few minutes later. Longarm told the men in the gully to keep an eye on the slope where the bushwhackers had been hidden, just in case their appearing to ride off was a trick. It didn't seem to be. No slugs came searching for Longarm and Salty as they emerged into the open.

It took an hour to patch up the wounded men and catch some of the scattered horses. By the time that was done, Longarm knew there was no chance of catching up to the outlaws. They'd had a good-sized lead already, except for the men who had been left behind to deal with the pursuit. The main body of the gang was long gone by now.

Salty came over to him and said, "Looky there." Longarm looked and saw a figure on horseback approaching from the east. He recognized the bulky shape and the high-crowned hat. Sheriff Andy Finch had returned, as

Longarm had thought he might, but not until the shooting was well over.

Longarm watched in disgust as the sheriff approached. Finch took his hat off, waved it over his head, and called out, "Everybody all right?"

Longarm waved him on in, and when Finch reined his horse to a halt, he looked around in dismay at the wounded men, as well as the two corpses.

"Oh, Lordy," the sheriff said. "Look at what they done. That's Gil Sterling and Hamp Montgomery. Two o' Casa Grande's best citizens. They ain't . . . ain't . . ." Finch couldn't bring himself to say it.

"They're dead," Longarm finished for him. "We've got several more men who were hit, but I think they'll be all right."

"You got horses, I see. We better get started. We can make it back to town by dark."

Longarm knew it was petty, but he couldn't resist goading the sheriff. "We're not going after those outlaws?"

Finch's face darkened. "I want them sons o' bitches brought to justice just as much as you do, Parker. Probably more, because I'm a lawman and you're just a saddle tramp with a fast gun. But I got a responsibility to those men who are hurt. They were duly deputized, and I got to look out for 'em."

"What about the ones who are dead?"

"If you know how to raise the dead, then go to it, mister," Finch snapped. "You got my blessin'."

Longarm shrugged and turned away. He knew Finch was right. He was just angry and frustrated. He had been close to a few members of the gang he was after, but they had gotten away.

There would be a next time, he told himself. He would travel with Horton and Glorieta McCall on to Gila Bend and Yuma and then up the Colorado River. Chances were, he would be on hand, or at least close by, when the bullion gang struck again.

And next time, the outcome would be different, he promised himself. He couldn't raise the dead—but he could do his damnedest to even the score for them.

It was almost nightfall by the time the posse returned to Casa Grande. Their pace on the trip back had been slowed by the wounded men. Jerome Horton came out of the Southwestern Freighting and Express Company office next to the barn as the posse rode slowly down the street.

"You didn't catch them?" he asked as he hurried up to Longarm, Salty, and Sheriff Finch.

"No, sir, I'm sorry to say we didn't," Finch replied. "All we caught was a heap o' trouble. Those bastards bushwhacked us. Killed two members of my posse and wounded some others."

"My God," Horton muttered. "They've really gone on a killing spree."

Longarm reined in and swung down wearily from the saddle. "Sorry we weren't able to get that bullion back," he said to Horton. "Any trouble here?"

"From Aragones, you mean?" Horton shook his head. "Carl has been guarding Glorieta, but no one has bothered her. In fact, I haven't seen Aragones or any of his men all day. They may have pulled out and headed back to the rancho."

That possibility worried Longarm a little. Horton might decide that he no longer needed Longarm's services as a bodyguard for Glorieta. That would mean he'd have to find some other excuse for hanging around this part of the territory.

Horton scotched that idea in a hurry. "Even if Aragones is gone, though, I don't believe we've seen the last of him. I don't trust him any farther than I could throw him.

I'll want you to stay on, Mr. Parker, just in case there's any more trouble."

Longarm nodded. "That's fine by me. I want to wash off some of this trail dust, and then I'll be ready to get back to work. I reckon we'll be staying one more night in Casa Grande after all?"

"Of course. It's much too late to start for Gila Bend now. I've wired ahead that we'll be delayed by a day from our original schedule."

Despite the killings and the loss of the bullion, Horton was still thinking about Glorieta McCall's singing career. The man's interests were seriously divided, Longarm thought.

He headed for the hotel, asking the clerk on his way through the lobby to see about having a bathtub and some hot water brought up. The clerk nodded, eager to comply with anything one of Jerome Horton's employees wanted. Longarm went upstairs, and in short order, a porter arrived with a bathtub, followed by a couple of maids, each carrying two buckets full of steaming hot water that they emptied into the tub.

"You can go ahead and get started on your bath, Mr. Parker," the porter told Longarm. "I'll be back in a few minutes with a couple more buckets o' water."

"Much obliged," Longarm said. When the porter and the maids were gone, he took off his gunbelt, coiled it, and placed it on a chair next to the tub where the Colt would be handy if he needed it. Then he stripped off his dusty clothes, tossed them in a corner of the room, and stepped into the tub. The water was hot enough to make him wince a little as he lowered himself into it, but then he sighed as he felt the heat begin to work its magic on his sore, tired muscles. He sunk as low as he could in the big, galvanized tub and leaned back to close his eyes.

A few minutes later, he was about to doze off when there was a soft knock on the door of the room. Instantly,

Longarm's hand moved so that it hovered over the butt of the revolver on the chair next to him. "Who is it?"

"Got them buckets of hot water for you, Mr. Parker," the porter called through the door.

"All right, bring 'em on in." Longarm relaxed and closed his eyes again.

He heard the door open and then close. Footsteps came across the room toward him, barely audible because of the thick rug on the floor. First one bucket and then the other were poured into the tub, making the water even hotter and raising the level until it was almost to Longarm's chin. He murmured, "*Gracias.*"

"*De nada,*" a woman's voice said. Then a hand reached under the water and found his crotch. Soft fingers closed around his manhood.

Longarm's eyes flew open, and it required quite an effort of his iron will to keep him from exploding up out of the water with a startled yell. Glorieta McCall knelt beside the tub, the sleeves of her dressing gown pushed up so they wouldn't get wet as she reached into the water. The hand holding Longarm's shaft caressed it firmly, causing it to grow hard in her palm, while the other rubbed across his bare, wet chest, fingers stroking the thick mat of dark brown hair that grew there. She smiled and continued her caresses as she leaned forward to kiss him.

Her lips were soft, hot, and sweet. Longarm enjoyed tasting them. But eventually his curiosity got the better of him. He pulled back a little to ask, "How'd you get in here? I thought that porter was bringin' the water."

"For five dollars, he was more than happy to let me take over the job. He was even willing to answer for me when you called out. I had to promise him that he wouldn't get in trouble, though." She pumped her hand up and down on his erect organ. "You're not upset with him for helping me, are you?"

"Not hardly," Longarm said. His voice was hoarse now, and he had a little trouble getting the words out. Glorieta was having quite an effect on him.

"Let's get all this dust off you. I'm tired of waiting, Custis. I want you."

Longarm wanted her, too, but he didn't care for the idea of Horton busting in on them. "What about—" he started to say.

She shook her head, obviously reading his mind. Or maybe it was just feminine intuition. "Jerome is down at his office. I don't expect him back for hours. And you don't have to worry, Custis. I told you there's nothing romantic between Jerome and me. We're not lovers. He really is like a father to me."

Well, Longarm thought, if people were going to keep telling him that, he supposed he might as well believe it. Especially considering what Glorieta was doing to him.

"If you're going to wash me," he said with a grin, "you might want to take that gown off. I might get to splashin' a mite."

She returned the grin and stood up. "All right," she said as she untied the gown's belt. She shrugged out of the garment, letting it fall off of her arms and around her hips to puddle on the floor around her feet. She was nude underneath it, and every bit as lovely as Longarm had expected her to be. Her breasts were full, firm, and rounded, perfect globes of creamy flesh crowned with hard, pink nipples. Below her breasts, her flat belly flowed flawlessly into the swell of her hips, which then curved into sleek thighs and calves. The triangle of fine-spun hair that covered her mound was the same dark red shade as her hair.

Glorieta dropped to her knees and began washing Longarm with a cloth that had been draped over the side of the tub. He luxuriated in her touch, closing his eyes again in pure enjoyment. When she was finished, she said, "Stand up, and I'll dry you."

Longarm stood, water sluicing down over his hard-muscled body. His shaft jutted out proudly from his groin. Glorieta picked up a fluffy towel from the bed where the porter had left it and started drying him. The thick, slightly rough towel and the expert probing of her fingers eased the last of the stiffness out of his muscles . . . except for one. It was as hard as a bar of iron.

When Glorieta came to it, her touch became softer, more gentle, but still arousing. He stepped out of the tub and she knelt in front of him to dry his legs. Her face was right in front of his groin. She leaned closer so that she could stroke her cheek along the length of him. His shaft throbbed as he felt the warmth of her breath on it.

She opened her mouth and slid her lips over the head of his manhood. He was so long and thick she could take only part of his shaft into her mouth. Her tongue swirled tantalizingly around the crown, then her lips closed around him and she began to suck.

Longarm suppressed the urge to spend right then and there. It would have been easy to empty himself into her mouth. But he wanted more than that, and he suspected Glorieta did, too. For a few minutes, he let himself thoroughly enjoy what she was doing to him. Then he put his hands on her shoulders and urged her to her feet.

Drawing her into his embrace, he kissed her soundly, sending his tongue into her mouth to explore the hot, wet cavern. Her hands clutched at him. He slid his hands down her back to cup the firm hemispheres of her rump and press her more closely against him. After a few moments, she began backing toward the bed. Longarm went with her without breaking the kiss.

Their lips didn't part until Glorieta sprawled back on the bed, opening her thighs. Her dark red hair spread out on the pillow under her head. She was perfect, a vision by lamplight. Longarm moved between her thighs and reached down to stroke the folds of flesh at the entrance to her core. They were slick with the heated moisture welling up from inside her. Longarm's thumb found the hard nubbin of flesh just below her mound and strummed it, causing her hips to surge up off the bed.

"I need you in me, Custis!" she gasped. "I need you deep inside me."

Longarm brought the head of his shaft to her opening. Just on general principles, he hated not to oblige a lady's request, especially this one. His hips drove forward, and his shaft slid easily into her, filling her.

Glorieta's arms went around his neck and pulled his head down to hers so that she could kiss him again. Her breasts flattened against his chest as his weight pinned her to the bed and he began stroking in and out of her. She wrapped her legs around his hips. He felt the strength of her thighs as she drew him even closer to her.

For long minutes he pistoned into her. At the same time, their tongues were fighting a fierce duel, thrusting and darting and swooping around each other. Longarm slid his hands under her hips and lifted her so that he could delve even deeper into her. She met him evenly, giving as good as she was getting. It was as close to pure perfection as the joining of male and female could achieve.

When Longarm felt his climax boiling up, he didn't try to hold back. Glorieta was panting against his mouth and giving out little mewling cries of passion, and he knew she was as close to the brink as he was. He drew back and then sheathed himself fully, probing her innermost recesses. His seed burst from him in spasm after shuddering spasm. He emptied himself into her, filling her to overflowing as her spasms told him that she had reached her own culmination, too.

They lay there like that for a moment, covered with a fine sheen of sweat and still joined, before Longarm withdrew and rolled onto his side next to Glorieta. He wrapped his arms around her as she snuggled against him. Longarm stroked her hair. She said, "My God, Custis, that was wonderful. I never . . . Custis?"

When he didn't respond, she lifted her head to look at him, but Longarm didn't know it. The long ride, the lack of sleep, the hot bath, and the vigorous lovemaking had all taken their toll.

Longarm was fast asleep.

Chapter 5

When Longarm woke up the next morning, he was as
ravenous as a bear following a long winter's hibernation.
He didn't remember anything from the night before except
making love with Glorieta McCall. He reached out and
felt that she wasn't in bed with him. Sitting up, he blinked
several times and looked around the room, which was lit
up by sunlight slanting through the gauzy curtains. No
sign of Glorieta. The bathtub was still there, though. The
water in it would be pretty tepid by now.

Longarm tousled his hair and yawned. He hadn't been
aware of it at all when Glorieta slipped out of bed and
left the room. Sleeping that soundly was unusual for
him—and a mite disturbing. His lawman's instincts
should have kept him from going that far under. A fella
who packed a badge had to learn how to sleep light. Why,
she could have cut his throat if she'd been of a mind to!

But since she hadn't, Longarm supposed she had been
satisfied by their romping. He grinned at the memory as
he swung his legs out of bed and stood up to get dressed.

When he came down into the lobby a few minutes later,
a voice hailed him from the hotel dining room. Longarm
walked through the arched entrance and saw Salty sitting

59

at a table with a huge stack of flapjacks in front of him. There was also a platter piled high with bacon, sausage, and eggs, as well as a bowl full of biscuits, a gravy boat, a jar of molasses, and a coffeepot. Salty waved Longarm over. "Be obliged if you'd join me," the old-timer greeted him. "You'll have to get your own breakfast, though."

Longarm grinned as he took one of the empty chairs and dropped his hat on another one. "What time does the rest of the army get here?" he asked.

"Don't make fun o' your elders, boy. Drivin' a stage-coach is hard work. A man works up a powerful hunger. And the grub you get at the relay stations ain't always fit to eat."

Longarm knew that to be true. He caught the eye of a plump, pretty waitress and pointed to the food Salty had, then to himself. She gave him a weak smile and nodded her understanding. Longarm hoped the cook had plenty of provisions on hand back there in the kitchen.

Longarm looked around at the dining room with its polished wooden tables and fancy place settings. "No of-fense, Salty, but this don't strike me as the sort of place you'd usually chow down."

"It ain't," Salty agreed around a mouthful of flapjack. "But since I'm workin' special-like for Mr. Horton now, drivin' that coach for him and the gal, he told me to come over here and have breakfast this mornin', on him. I ain't foolish enough to pass up a free meal. The food ain't that much better'n what you can get at the hash house, but there's a whole heap more of it." The old man leaned toward Longarm and lowered his voice. "An' that saucy little waitress ain't bad, neither."

"You still notice things like that at your advanced age, Salty?"

The old-timer glowered across the table at Longarm. "I may be a mite long in the tooth, but there ain't nothin' wrong with my eyes! Nor any other part of me, neither!"

"I'll take your word for it," Longarm said with a grin.

A few minutes later, the waitress started bringing over his food. It took her several trips, and Salty eyed her appreciatively each time. Longarm dug in, washing down the food with several cups of strong black coffee. Salty had a head start and finished breakfast ahead of him, but not by much.

"Feel better?" the old man asked when they were both done eating.

"Reckon I'll live. Where's Horton this morning?"

"Down at the office goin' over a few last-minute details with Pete Kilmer. He's the fella who's gonna take over for me around here whilst I'm gone."

"What about Miss McCall?"

"Ain't seen her," Salty said with a shake of his head. "You're supposed to be guardin' her. Don't you know where she is?"

Longarm felt a stirring of alarm. Salty was right. He should have checked on Glorieta before coming down here to eat breakfast. He snatched his hat off the chair next to him and stood up. "I'll be right back."

His long legs carried him out of the dining room and up the stairs to the second floor. He knocked on the door of the suite where Glorieta and Horton were staying. There was no answer. Clearly worried now, Longarm reached down and grasped the knob. The frown on his face deepened when it turned freely in his hand. The door was unlocked.

He opened the door and stepped into the sitting room. The bedrooms opened one on each side. Longarm didn't know which one was Glorieta's. He moved to the door on the right and jerked it open. The room beyond was empty. Wheeling around, he went to the other door. He thought about calling out but didn't do it. If anybody was lurking in the suite who shouldn't be, Longarm didn't want to announce his identity. He grasped the knob of the left-hand door and jerked it open.

"My goodness!" Glorieta exclaimed. "You're not going to shoot me, are you, Custis?"

Longarm realized he was gripping the butt of his holstered Colt. He took his hand off the gun and shook his head. "Sorry for bargin' in on you like this. I got worried something might have happened to you. It's my job to look out for you, after all. Didn't you hear me knock?"

She was fully dressed and had been in the act of closing a valise on her bed when Longarm surprised her. Now she shook her head in response to his question and finished buckling the straps that held the luggage closed. "I'm afraid not, but it's all right that you came in," she said. "I feel better just knowing that you're around."

Several other pieces of luggage were stacked on the floor, including a good-sized trunk. "Is this all your stuff?" he asked.

"A girl can't travel as light as you men do," Glorieta said with a laugh. "Don't worry, there's plenty of room for it on the wagon."

"That's good, because I don't reckon it'd all fit in the stagecoach boot. I'll carry it down for you."

"No need for that. Jerome said he would send some men over from the freight office for it."

Longarm nodded. "You look like you're about ready to go."

"I am," she said, her expression growing more solemn. "Casa Grande is a nice enough town, I suppose, and I'm very grateful for the reception I received for my performances in Mr. Campanella's saloon. But there's been a lot of trouble here, too."

Thinking about the kidnapping attempt on her and the raid on the mule train that had left close to a dozen men dead, not to mention the ambush on the posse that had pursued the outlaws, Longarm nodded. "Maybe our luck will change in Gila Bend."

He would believe that, though, when he saw it.

It was a little before midmorning before the party of travelers finally got around to leaving. The stagecoach rolled out of Casa Grande with Salty perched on the driver's box, handling the reins of the six-horse hitch. The coach had once been a standard Concord, the sort of vehicle that had bounced on its wide leather thoroughbraces and rolled along dusty trails and through mountain passes all over the west. The red and yellow paint of the Overland Stagecoach Company had been replaced by a glossy black, and shiny silver fittings had replaced the more common brass ones. A double layer of curtains, canvas on the outside and fine linen on the inside, kept at least some of the dust from coming in the windows. Instead of plain benches, the coach was outfitted with polished hardwood seats covered with thick, comfortable cushions. Longarm had seen all that during a quick glance inside. It looked like a pleasant way to travel, all right.

Following the coach was a good-sized spring wagon with a canvas cover over its bed to protect the luggage. A stocky man named Augie Martinez drove it. Augie was short for Augusto, he had explained to Longarm when they were introduced just before the group left Casa Grande. His wife Blanca, who was as friendly as her husband, rode on the wagon seat beside him. She worked as Glorieta's maid.

Salty had invited Longarm to tie the buckskin behind the coach and ride on the driver's box with him, but Longarm declined. "I'll do that later," he promised. "I might want to scout ahead, get the lay of the land."

"Look for bushwhackers, you mean," Salty said.

Longarm just inclined his head and didn't really answer.

From Casa Grande to Gila Bend was about sixty miles. There were three relay stations between where they could switch teams, as part of an arrangement Horton had with the stage line that ran through this part of the territory. Despite the late start, Longarm expected to reach Gila Bend before nightfall. The coach could cover eight to ten miles per hour, though that pace would slow somewhat when it had to climb to the pass through the range of small mountains between the two settlements.

Longarm rode ahead to scout the trail, though he was careful not to get out of sight of the coach. The day was hot, dry, and windy, as usual for this part of the country. A few clouds dotted the sky to the north, teasing the thirsty land with the notion that they might drop a little rain. Even if it did rain, though, Longarm knew, most of the moisture would evaporate before it reached the ground. He had seen more than one Arizona thunderstorm play itself out high in the air without a single drop ever hitting the dust.

Seeing that everything seemed peaceful, he turned and rode back to join the coach and the wagon. He put the buckskin into a walk even with the back of the coach and stepped out of the saddle onto the rear boot. After tying the horse's reins to the silver rail around the top of the coach, he climbed up and over, making the vehicle rock a little. "Sorry!" he called down to Horton and Glorieta as he reached the driver's box and lowered himself to the seat beside Salty.

"Is everything all right?" Horton asked through the window on that side of the coach.

"Fine," Longarm replied. "I'm just resting my horse for a spell."

The day passed peacefully with Longarm riding on the coach part of the time and ranging ahead the rest of the time. He enjoyed talking to Salty. The old-timer had been to see the elephant, that was for sure. Most people would have taken the old man's stories of all the places he'd been and all the things he'd done with a grain of salt, but not Longarm. Salty dropped enough details into his yarns for Longarm to know that he was telling the truth. For the most part, anyway. Salty might have been exaggerating a mite now and then.

The only thing Salty didn't seem to want to talk about was his personal life. "I was married," he said in reply to a question. "Once. It didn't take." Longarm changed the subject and didn't bring it up again.

Fresh teams were waiting for them at each of the relay stations. Salty handled the horses expertly, and he negotiated the tricky trail through the mountain pass with ease. During that stretch of the trip, Longarm got his Winchester from the saddle boot and sat next to the old man with the rifle cocked and ready in his lap. Such terrain was made-to-order for anybody who wanted to stop a stagecoach, because the vehicle had to slow down as it climbed to the pass. Steep slopes closed in on both sides of the trail; and there were plenty of places for bushwhackers to hide.

No one bothered the travelers, though, and soon the coach was rolling down the other side of the pass, making good time for Gila Bend once more. The two vehicles reached the town about an hour before sunset.

The settlement was smaller than Casa Grande and was named for a sharp bend in the Gila River nearby. The river provided enough water so that a little farming went on, but mining and ranching were the main activities in the area. There was also a pretty nice saloon on the town's main street, Dempsey's Silver Kettle. The place was run by a burly, jovial Irishman named Connor Dempsey, and the kettle that gave the saloon its name stood on the end of the bar. Dempsey used it instead of a cash drawer, tossing customers' money into it and making change from it. It would have been easy to grab the kettle and make a run for the door, Longarm supposed, but people in Gila

Bend knew not to try it. A man with a dark, narrow face sat beside the door, a shotgun in his lap, and his eyes were alert under the brim of his derby hat. Anybody who tried to run off with the kettle would get a gutful of buckshot in a hurry, Longarm suspected.

He stood at the bar, sipping from a mug of beer while Horton introduced Glorieta to Dempsey and the saloon owner proudly showed her the stage on which she would sing that night. Dempsey had had a sign painted, too, announcing that the world famous Arizona Flame would perform at the Silver Kettle. The letters of Glorieta's name had little flames outlining them, which Longarm thought was a nice touch.

While Horton and Glorieta were busy, Longarm picked up his beer and strolled over to the front door. "Howdy," he said to the shotgun guard. "Seen anything of a fancy-dressed young Mexican fella around here, probably has at least a couple of vaqueros traveling with him?"

"Nope." The guard shook his head. "Ain't nobody like that been in here. And I'd know, 'cause I see everybody that comes in."

Longarm was willing to bet that was true. He drifted back to the bar and asked the same question of several men who stood there drinking, getting the same answer each time. Maybe Don Rafael Aragones really *had* given up and gone home to his papa's ranch across the border. Maybe he hadn't been behind the kidnapping attempt at all. Longarm wasn't ready to believe either of those things was true, but they were possibilities, at least.

There was a hotel in Gila Bend, but the rooms upstairs in the Silver Kettle were even better, Dempsey claimed. He seemed to be telling the truth, Longarm decided when he, Horton, and Glorieta went up to see where they would be staying. Blanca Martinez would also have a room at the Silver Kettle, so that she would be close by whenever Glorieta needed her to do anything. Salty and Augie would bed down at the livery barn where the coach and the wagon were parked, so that they could keep an eye on things overnight.

More men began to drift into the saloon soon after the sun went down. By the time Glorieta's performance was almost ready to begin, there was a large crowd in the room. Longarm scanned the faces of the men who had come to hear the Arizona Flame, but he didn't see anyone who looked familiar. There was no sign of Aragones.

Longarm hadn't forgotten the other reason—the real reason—he was here. He moved along the bar, pausing to chat with as many men as he could, and as he did so, he casually brought up the series of bullion robberies that had taken place to the east, the last one near Casa Grande. Most of the men had heard about the trouble. Quite a few of them were miners and were worried about what would happen if the thieves kept moving west, as they seemed to be doing. No one had any idea who was behind the raids, though.

Longarm had just finished one such conversation and was moving along the bar when a big hand reached across the hardwood and clamped itself around his wrist. He stopped and looked up into the eyes of Connor Dempsey. Those eyes were gray and were set in deep pits of gristle. Dempsey leaned closer and said in a voice that carried only to Longarm, "Ye seem mighty interested in the gold and silver shipments in these parts, bucko. Ye wouldn't be tryin' to gather information to pass along to some owl-hoot compadres of yours, now would ye?"

Longarm felt a flash of anger at being grabbed like that, but he controlled it. "I don't reckon you've heard the whole story," he said. "When that bunch of outlaws hit one of Horton's mule trains carryin' bullion into Casa Grande, I was a member of the posse that went after 'em."

"A mighty good way of throwin' suspicion off yourself, I'm thinkin'."

"And when they ambushed us, I came mighty damn

close to being ventilated," Longarm shot back. "You ask Salty or anybody else who was along if they think I was working with the bandits."

Dempsey frowned. "You're sayin' that Salty will vouch for ye?"

"I'd be mighty surprised if he didn't."

Dempsey let go of Longarm's wrist and raised his hand to rub his jaw. "That old rapscallion's one o' the best men I know. I reckon if he thinks you're all right, I'll go along with him. But how come you're so interested in them bullion holdups?"

"I'm working for Horton," Longarm said. "Not only that, I like him. These robberies are going to ruin his business if the gang pulling them isn't caught. And to cap it off, the sons of bitches shot at me. I don't like that, and I ain't goin' to forget about it any time soon."

A grin spread across Dempsey's rugged face. "Ah, now you're talkin' a language I can understand. Ye feel like ye have a score to settle with the spalpeens."

"That's right," Longarm said. "Horton hired me to keep Miss McCall safe, and that's what I intend to do. But if I can get a line on those owlhoots at the same time . . ."

"I know what ye mean. I'll keep me ear to the ground, and if I hear anything while you're here, I'll pass it along." Dempsey put out his hand. "Fair enough?"

"Fair enough," Longarm said as he shook hands with the big Irishman.

Glorieta came out a few minutes later to begin her performance. It was the third time Longarm had seen the show, but he was still enthralled. She was just that good at what she did, which seemed simple on the surface. She stood in the middle of the stage and sang while Dempsey's piano player accompanied her. And with nothing but her voice she wrapped a spell around every man in the room, transporting them out of their drab surroundings in southern Arizona to some sort of magical realm where every day was spring and anything was possible. Then, as she launched into a pensive ballad, she eased her listeners back into the past, bringing tears to the eyes of more than one man in the room as they thought of homes and loved ones long gone. There was something truly mystical about it, Longarm thought as he caught himself musing about his own past loves, all the way back to his West Virginia boyhood. A grin tugged at his mouth. Glorieta was good, damned good.

When she concluded her performance, the applause wasn't as loud as it had been at the Golden Horde in Casa Grande only because Dempsey's Silver Kettle was somewhat smaller and couldn't hold as many men. But the reaction of the audience was every bit as enthusiastic. The men hooted and hollered and banged their hands together and stamped their feet until Glorieta came out for her encore. Longarm drifted backstage while she was singing that final song.

She was smiling when she ducked through the curtains and came running over to him. "They liked me!" she said.

"Well, of course they did," Longarm told her. "You're probably the prettiest gal they've seen in years, if not ever, and I reckon nobody who could sing like you ever came to Gila Bend before."

Laughing, Glorieta threw her arms around Longarm's neck and hugged him. "It feels so good!" she said, delighting in the reaction to her performance.

Longarm knew that Horton would be coming backstage at any moment. He was convinced now that Glorieta was telling the truth about the two of them not being lovers, but he still didn't want to make Horton jealous. There was no way of knowing what might be in the back of the man's mind. He unwound Glorieta's arms from his neck, gave her a quick kiss, and then squeezed her hands as he stepped back. Sure enough, Horton came bustling backstage a moment later, followed by a beaming Connor

Dempsey. The burly Irishman used the back of his massive hand to wipe tears away from his eyes.

"Ah, lass!" Dempsey said. "Ye have the sweetest voice that I've ever heard! 'Twas like ye had carried me back to the land o' me birth."

Horton hugged Glorieta and kissed her cheek. "That was excellent! Just splendid! You see, my dear, when I first met you in Ah Wong's and told you that you were destined for much greater things, I was right."

"I owe it all to you, Jerome," she murmured. "I can never repay you for what you've done for me."

"It's no more than you've done for me. You've made me feel young again, Glorieta. I'm so proud of you."

Longarm stood back and watched. He was glad Horton had something that made him feel so good, but at the same time, the man should have been concentrating more on those robberies that threatened to bankrupt him. If enough of those gold and silver shipments were lost to the bandits, it might even have an effect on the country's economy sooner or later, according to Billy Vail.

But nothing was going to intrude on this moment for Horton. With his arm around Glorieta's shoulders, he said, "Let's go upstairs and have dinner. Connor's cook has prepared a special meal for us."

"All right."

Longarm didn't figure he was invited, but Horton paused and looked over his shoulder to say, "Aren't you coming, Mr. Parker?"

"You want me along?" Longarm asked, surprised.

"I certainly do. I haven't forgotten about what happened in Casa Grande, and I certainly don't trust Rafael Aragones." Horton looked down at Glorieta. "I'm sorry to bring up that unpleasant memory, my dear, but we must be practical."

"That's all right, Jerome." Glorieta smiled at Longarm. "I enjoy Mr. Parker's company, too."

And she dropped one eyelid in a meaningful wink that no one except Longarm could see.

Longarm smiled back at her, but he had to suppress a sigh. He was willing to eat supper with Glorieta and Horton, but he sure hoped she didn't go to playing footsie with him under the table, or anything scandalous like that.

Chapter 6

It was twice as far from Gila Bend to Yuma as it was from Casa Grande to Gila Bend, so it took two days to reach the town in the southwestern corner of Arizona Territory, on the Colorado River. That was two days of hot, dusty travel through a flat, arid, mostly featureless landscape. Other than a few scrubby bushes here and there, there was no vegetation to speak of. An occasional mesa or small mountain poked up from the desert, barely breaking the monotony. Longarm was damned glad when the stagecoach and the wagon reached the bluff overlooking the winding river and the town perched on its southern bank.

He shouldn't complain too much about the trip, though, he told himself. At least there hadn't been any trouble. No sign of Aragones or anybody else who wanted to bother them.

Horton leaned out one of the coach windows and called up to Salty, "Drive directly to the riverboat landing. We'll be staying on the *Manatee*."

"Sure thing, Mr. Horton," Salty replied. When Horton had ducked back into the coach, the old-timer leaned closer to Longarm and said in lower tones, "I've always wondered—what the hell kind of a name is *Manatee*?"

"It's a critter that lives in the ocean, down around Florida and the islands in the Caribbean Sea," Longarm explained.

"You mean some kind o' fish?"

"No, it's a mammal. Some folks call 'em sea cows, because they look sort of like a cow only with little bitty front legs and no back legs at all, just a big ol' flipperlike sort of thing."

Salty stared at Longarm. "You're makin' that up! There ain't no such animal. Couldn't be."

"I've seen them with my own eyes," Longarm said with a solemn nod.

"Well, I never heard of such nonsense. Who'd name a riverboat after a made-up animal?"

"I reckon maybe we'll find out. And it *ain't* made-up."

Salty just snorted skeptically.

At this point, the Colorado was a wide, dark blue stream that wound between high, rust-colored bluffs as it ran in a generally northsouth direction, forming the border between Arizona and California. Its headwaters were in the Rockies, not all that far from Longarm's home base of Denver. The stream flowed southwestward through a corner of Utah and into northern Arizona, where it had carved out a huge canyon. After turning south, the Colorado ran all the way across the Mexican border to empty into the Gulf of California.

Longarm was quite familiar with the river, his job having taken him to many different points along it, from its mountain beginnings all the way to the Gulf. He had been to Yuma several times, too. The superintendent of the famous—or infamous—prison located there knew him well. Longarm didn't intend to go anywhere near the prison on this trip, though. He would be sticking close to Horton and Glorieta, which meant he'd be on the riverboat and at the opera house where Glorieta would be singing.

He planned on staying behind the scenes as much as possible, so that he would be less likely to run into anybody who might recognize him as a deputy U.S. marshal.

Salty drove the coach straight through town to the riverboat landing. The Colorado was the only river in this part of the country large enough for paddle wheelers. It was navigable all the way up to Hardyville, a mining town about a hundred and fifty miles north of Yuma, located across the river from the spot where California and Nevada came together. It wasn't unusual to see several riverboats tied up at the Yuma landing. They did a brisk traffic up and down the Colorado, carrying supplies in and gold and silver out.

"Does Horton own the boat we're going on?" Longarm asked Salty as the old-timer brought the coach to a stop near the wharves that jutted out into the river. The timber to build the docks had had to be freighted in by wagon from California or northern Arizona. There were no trees big enough down in this part of the territory to form such heavy beams.

"He owns most of it, I reckon. I think the fella who's the captain has got a share, too. I never met him. I don't get over this way very often. He's supposed to be an English feller, or some sort of foreigner, anyway." Salty grunted. "Reckon he's prob'ly the one who come up with the funny name."

The *Manatee* might have a funny name, but it was a fine-looking riverboat, a well-kept-up stern-wheeler with three decks stacked like the layers of a wedding cake and topped by a pilothouse. The last time Longarm had been on a riverboat, it had been a long way north of here, he recalled, in the Alaska Territory. He hoped there wouldn't be as much trouble on this voyage as there had been on the *Yukon Queen*.

Horton opened the coach door and stepped out, then turned around to help Glorieta down from the vehicle.

Longarm and Salty dropped to the ground from the driver's box. Augie Martinez pulled the wagon up right behind the coach.

Yuma was a bigger town than Casa Grande and Gila Bend put together, but it wasn't very impressive. Most of the buildings were low, flat-roofed adobes, with only a few frame structures downtown housing businesses. Adobe warehouses lined the riverbank near the landing. In the distance loomed the high walls of the dreaded territorial prison. It was a harsh place, Longarm knew, if not quite the hellhole some people made it out to be. Many men had tried to escape from the prison over the years, but few had made it. Of those who actually got outside the walls, the desert claimed the lives of most of them.

Obviously, Horton's party was expected. A man in a blue jacket and black cap stepped out of the pilothouse, lifted a hand in greeting, and then started down the steep, narrow ladders to the main deck. When he reached it, he came across a plank walkway connecting the deck to the landing and extended his hand to Horton. "Jerome! Wonderful to see you again!" The man had a bit of an accent, but it didn't sound English to Longarm.

Horton shook hands with the riverboat captain. "Hello, Henry. How are you?"

"Couldn't be better." The captain was medium height and stockily built, with graying dark hair under his cap and a neatly trimmed mustache. His clothes, rather than wilting in the heat, were crisp and pressed, with hardly any dust on them. Like his boat, everything about the captain seemed to be neat.

Horton turned to Glorieta. "And this is the lady you've heard so much about. Miss Glorieta McCall, Captain Henry James O'Brien."

"At your service, ma'am," Captain. O'Brien said. He swept his hat off his head and gave a little bow. Longarm wondered if he was going to kiss the back of Glorieta's hand, but he didn't go that far. He just shook it instead.

Horton motioned Longarm forward. "This is Custis Parker, who's traveling with us." He didn't explain why Longarm was with the group, but surely he would later. The captain had the right to know that there might be trouble on his boat.

O'Brien's handshake was firm. "Pleased to meet you, Parker." The man's keen gray eyes narrowed a little. "You have the look of a seagoing man about you, sir."

"Not hardly," Longarm replied with a grin, thinking of the times he'd been shanghaied while working on various cases and wound up working as a virtual slave on ships captained by brutal killers. He had almost lost his life on those ships and had no desire to go back to sea.

"Well, perhaps not, though I suspect a man such as yourself would fit in no matter where fate chose to take you. I'm from Canada myself, Ontario, but I think of myself as a citizen of the world now, since I've traveled so much of it." O'Brien turned and indicated the gangplank with a wave of his hand. "Shall we go aboard?"

Horton motioned for Glorieta to go first. She walked onto the boat, followed by Horton, Longarm, and Captain O'Brien. Salty, Augie, and Blanca waited with the stagecoach and the wagon. Once the rest were aboard, O'Brien signaled to a tall, muscular, rawboned man with a craggy face.

"My first mate," O'Brien explained. "Joe Cleghorn. He's sailed with me from Singapore to Newfoundland. He'll see to it that the deckhands bring all the bags aboard. Now, if you'll come with me, Miss McCall . . ." O'Brien offered Glorieta his arm, which she took with a smile. "I'll show you to your accommodations."

The passengers' cabins were on the second deck. O'Brien took Glorieta and Horton to adjoining cabins on the starboard side of the riverboat, then turned to Longarm and said, "Your cabin will be around on the port side, Mr. Parker."

Glorieta had gone into her cabin to look around, but Horton was still standing there on the deck. When he heard what the captain said to Longarm, he frowned. "I'm sorry, Henry, but that won't do," he said. "Mr. Parker's room has to be closer than that, right next door to us if that's possible."

"And why is that?" O'Brien asked bluntly.

Horton looked around and then said in a quiet voice, "Because he's working for me as Miss McCall's bodyguard. Someone tried to kidnap her in Casa Grande."

O'Brien's eyebrows arched. "Is that so? That's very interesting, Jerome. And you think the young lady may still be in danger?"

"I wouldn't rule it out," Horton said.

"So you believe there may be trouble here on the *Manatee*?"

"I was going to tell you all about it, Henry," Horton said, somewhat defensively. "I planned to wait until we were having a drink in your cabin, though."

O'Brien crossed his arms over his chest. "Well, a man doesn't sail the briny deep without courage. If trouble comes, we'll meet it head-on."

"That's exactly what I was hoping you'd say," Horton replied with a relieved smile.

O'Brien turned toward the row of doors that led into the cabins on the starboard side of the boat. "The cabin next to yours is already occupied," he said. "We do have other passengers for this trip, you know. But there's the vacant one on the port side where I planned to put Mr. Parker. I'll see if the fellow in this cabin would mind switching." The captain went to the door of the cabin in question and rapped sharply on it.

A moment later, the door was opened by a dark-haired, handsome young man who wore expensive trousers, a white silk shirt with ruffles on the front, and highly polished boots. A silk tie was looped around his neck, but the collar of his shirt was still unfastened and the tie wasn't tied yet. Obviously, he was getting ready for a night on the town or in the boat's salon.

"I hate to disturb you, Mr. Branch," O'Brien said. "I was wondering if you'd mind moving to another cabin, over on the port side of the boat. It would be every bit as comfortable as these accommodations, I assure you."

The young man frowned slightly. "I was already settled in, Captain . . ."

At that moment, Glorieta stepped back out of her cabin and began, "It looks very nice—" She stopped short and looked over at the young man called Branch. "Oh, I'm sorry. I didn't mean to interrupt what you were saying. Please, go on, sir."

Branch smiled. "I was just telling the captain how much I like the quarters on this side of the boat." The bold manner in which his eyes played over Glorieta's figure brought a frown to Horton's face, Longarm noticed. As he had thought, Horton was not above feeling jealous when another man paid too much attention to Glorieta, whether he was romantically interested in her or not.

Horton stepped forward and cleared his throat. "My name is Jerome Horton," he said. "I'm one of the owners of this vessel, along with Captain O'Brien. I'd take it as a personal favor, Mr. Branch, if you'd be willing to change cabins."

Branch took his eyes off Glorieta—reluctantly—and shrugged. "I suppose it wouldn't be too much bother."

"Excellent! To show my appreciation, I'd like for you to be my guest at the Yuma Opera House tonight."

"The Opera House," Branch repeated. "I seem to remember hearing something about some girl singing there . . ."

Horton nodded toward Glorieta. "That's Miss McCall. The world famous Arizona Flame."

Branch looked at her again, and the smile on his face widened. "I see. In that case, I'll certainly accept your kind invitation, Mr. Horton. If Miss McCall sings half as beautifully as she looks, it will be an entertaining evening indeed."

Longarm was only halfway paying attention to the conversation. Something was familiar about this young fella called Branch. Longarm seemed to recognize him from somewhere, but the big lawman was damned if he could recall where.

"I can give up cards for one evening," Branch went on, still smiling at Glorieta.

"You're a card player?" Horton asked.

"That's how I make my living," Branch murmured.

So Branch was a professional gambler. And a successful one, from the looks of his clothes. Longarm had run into plenty of tinhorns in his life, and he supposed it was possible he had sat across a poker table from Branch in some saloon somewhere. That was why the youngster looked familiar.

"I'll send a man to move your luggage for you," O'Brien said.

Branch shook his head. "Not necessary. I have only one bag. I travel light." He nodded politely to Glorieta. "I'll see you this evening, Miss McCall. I'm looking forward to it."

"Thank you," she said. "I hope you're not disappointed."

"I'm sure I won't be."

Horton cleared his throat again and took Glorieta's arm. "Come along, my dear, let's get you settled in." They went into Glorieta's cabin, and Horton closed the door behind them.

80

Branch looked at Longarm. "Are you the one who's getting my cabin?"

"Afraid so. Sorry to put you out, old son."

The gambler shrugged again. "One cabin's pretty much like another. The only reason I hesitated was so I'd have an excuse to look at that girl a little longer. Is she any good?"

"What?" Longarm asked with a frown.

"As a singer. Is she any good?"

"Oh. Voice like an angel, I reckon. Like an angel ought to sound, anyway."

"Well, then, I really am looking forward to attending her performance at the Opera House." The young man held out his hand. "Tyler Branch."

"Custis Parker," Longarm introduced himself as he returned Branch's handshake.

"And just what's your role in this little entourage?"

"I look out for Miss McCall."

Branch's gaze touched meaningfully on the holstered Colt at Longarm's hip. "Has there been trouble requiring the services of a man such as yourself, Mr. Parker?"

"Let's just say I'm here to make sure there ain't any such trouble."

Branch nodded slowly. "An ounce of prevention, eh? Well, I'll get out of your way. Your can have the cabin in just a few minutes. I was about ready to go to the salon for a drink, anyway. Maybe I'll see you there."

"Could be," Longarm said. "And much obliged for your cooperation."

"*De nada,*" Branch said, showing that despite his dudish-looking exterior, he had been in the West long enough to pick up some of the place's habits.

A few minutes later, Branch left the cabin, carrying a small carpetbag. He was wearing a frock coat and a flat-crowned black hat and looked more like a gambler than ever. Longarm was leaning on the rail at the edge of the deck. Branch gave him a pleasant nod as he went by, which Longarm returned.

Longarm's eyes narrowed, though, as he watched the young man's retreating back. For some reason, he sure wished he could remember where he had seen Tyler Branch before.

The cabins on board the *Manatee* were a lot nicer than the benches in the stagecoach relay station where they had spent the previous night, although not as luxurious or comfortable as the rooms at the Ames House in Casa Grande or Dempsey's Silver Kettle in Gila Bend. Longarm put his warbag and Winchester on the bunk, then went back out on deck to watch the unloading of the rest of the baggage. Salty waved to him from the wharf. Longarm gave the old man a lazy wave in return.

The door of Glorieta's cabin opened, and Horton came out on deck. "Miss McCall is going to rest for a while before we go to the Opera House," he said.

The sun had just set behind the mountains to the west, and dusk was beginning to drape itself over Yuma. Lamps were lit in the buildings, providing a warm yellow glow in the shadows. The breeze picked up a little, though the air was still hot. The dry desert atmosphere would cool off quickly, though, Longarm knew. By morning, there would be a chill in the air.

Longarm's eyes roved over the buildings closest to the river as he leaned on the railing. He stiffened and straightened from his casual pose as he spotted a man in a high-crowned sombrero lounging in the shadows next to an adobe building. Strains of guitar music drifted from the place, telling Longarm that it was probably a cantina. Which meant that it was perfectly reasonable to see a Mexican vaquero hanging around outside.

But Longarm remembered the two men who had been with Don Rafael Aragones. He couldn't tell if the man he saw now was one of those vaqueros, but it was certainly possible. That would mean Aragones had followed them to Yuma—or gotten ahead of them somehow.

"Something wrong, Parker?" Horton asked, taking note of Longarm's attitude.

"I don't know," Longarm muttered. "Could be one of Aragones's men over yonder, keepin' an eye on the boat." He nodded toward the vaquero without being too obvious about it.

Horton looked where Longarm indicated and exclaimed, "Damn it! I think you're right. That means he's still after Glorieta."

"If Aragones were responsible for what happened in Casa Grande in the first place."

"Yes, of course, of course." Horton sounded like he considered any other possibility too far-fetched to be taken seriously. And he was probably right about that, Longarm thought. Horton went on, "I'll want you to stay especially close to Glorieta tonight, Mr. Parker."

"Yes, sir," Longarm said, thinking of how close he'd been to Glorieta back in Casa Grande. Horton didn't know about that, and probably it would be a good idea if the incident wasn't repeated, Longarm thought with some regret. As sweet as Glorieta was, carrying on with her just complicated matters. And Longarm still had some bullion thieves to find.

An hour later, they left for the Opera House, Salty driving the short distance in the coach with Longarm riding on top beside him. Longarm kept his eyes open and looked suspiciously at every man he saw wearing a sombrero. He didn't see Don Rafael Aragones, but that didn't mean anything, he told himself. If Aragones was in Yuma and was still after Glorieta, he could be lying low while he sent his men to do the dirty work for him.

Arriving at the Opera House, Glorieta, Horton, and Longarm went in a rear entrance. The place was run by

83

an entrepreneur named Thaddeus Bowman, who had once been a prospector for gold and silver before making his fortune another way, by bringing entertainment to the citizens of Yuma. Bowman greeted them backstage.

"We've got a full house out there," he said happily. "And they're all anxious to hear you sing, Miss McCall."

"I just hope I don't let them down," Glorieta said worriedly.

Horton squeezed her hand. "Nonsense. You're going to do just fine."

Glorieta nodded but still looked a little nervous.

She didn't have anything to worry about. Longarm watched from the wings as Glorieta went on stage and sang her heart out, just as she had in Casa Grande and Gila Bend. The audience in the Opera House, which was as packed as Bowman had said, went wild after each song. Glorieta seemed to gain confidence as she went along, and by the time she finished her encore, the applause from the audience threatened to bring the place down. Longarm grinned as he watched her accepting the accolades.

Before the show started, Longarm had peeked through a gap in the curtains and seen no sign of Aragones in the audience. Tyler Branch was there, though, in the front row. Horton had been serious about paying him back for the inconvenience of changing cabins on the riverboat. Now, Longarm moved over a little in the wings so that he could see the front row of the audience. Branch was applauding like everyone else, but he had a certain reserve about him. Unlike the miners and cowboys who had packed into the Opera House to see and hear Glorieta, maybe a gambler and man of the world like Branch considered himself a mite too sophisticated to hoot and holler.

When Glorieta left the stage, Horton embraced her and congratulated her on another very successful performance. Glorieta was flushed and breathing a little hard from the emotions running through her. She accepted Horton's congratulations with a smile.

"I need to stay here for a while and discuss business with Mr. Bowman," Horton told her. "Would you like to wait, or would you rather go back to the riverboat?"

"I believe I'd rather go back to the boat, Jerome," she replied. "I'm tired, and I was thinking of having a bite of supper in the cabin and then going to bed."

Horton kissed her on the forehead. "That's fine. Mr. Parker will escort you."

Glorieta turned to Longarm with a smile, and he thought he saw mischief lurking in her green eyes. Maybe she wasn't as tired as she made out and had in mind a little romping with him when they got back to the boat. Longarm had told himself that wasn't a good idea, but he wasn't sure if he could resist Glorieta's charms. He was only human, after all.

When Glorieta had put on her hat and the short jacket she wore over her gown, Longarm linked arms with her and walked her out to the stagecoach. Salty was already on the box, waiting to drive them to the landing. The old-timer grinned down at Glorieta and said, "Hope you don't mind, but I snuck into the back o' the hall, ma'am. You sure sung mighty pretty."

"Why, thank you, Salty," she said. "I didn't know you had any interest in music."

"Well, I don't know nothin' about it, I reckon, but I know what I like when I hear it, and you sing mighty fine."

Longarm helped Glorieta into the coach and joined her there, sitting opposite her on the seat facing backward. No sooner had Salty gotten the vehicle in motion than Glorieta switched seats, moving over to settle herself next to Longarm. She snuggled against him and turned her face up for a kiss.

Longarm didn't figure it would hurt anything, since the

interior of the coach was dark. He kissed her for several long moments, relishing the sweet, wet heat of her mouth. Her hand went to his crotch and began to massage his stiffening organ through his trousers.

Damn it, Longarm thought. And he'd had such good intentions. But what was that old saying about the road to hell . . . ?

That was when Longarm heard a thump and then a pained grunt from the driver's box. The coach lurched suddenly, throwing him and Glorieta roughly to one side. The team started running harder, and hoofbeats sounded from both sides as galloping riders moved up to flank the now madly careening stagecoach. Longarm knew that Salty wasn't responsible for this wild ride. Somebody must have jumped the old man, knocked him out, and taken the reins. There was only one reason for anybody to do that: to get to Glorieta.

And this time, Longarm was being kidnapped right along with her.

Chapter 7

Glorieta let out a scream as the coach lurched around another corner and threw her and Longarm back the other way. Longarm grabbed her shoulder to steady her and pushed her toward the floor. Things were liable to get a mite hot in here, and he wanted her out of the line of fire as much as possible. "Stay down!" he told her as he drew his Colt and yanked the curtains aside over one of the windows.

The sharp turns meant that the coach was no longer heading toward the riverboat landing. Instead, it was racing out into the desert to the south of the settlement. Toward the Mexican border, Longarm thought. That was one more clue pointing to the manicured hand of Don Rafael Aragones being behind this.

The riders galloping alongside the stagecoach were just indistinct shapes in the darkness, but Longarm could tell they wore sombreros. Probably there were vaqueros behind the coach, too, escorting it away from Yuma. Longarm thought about taking a few potshots at the riders, but with the coach bouncing and jolting like it was, hitting anything would be difficult. Besides, the vaqueros would be under orders not to fire into the coach, for fear of hitting Glorieta, and to Longarm's way of thinking, ventilating an hombre who couldn't shoot back wasn't much better than murder.

He decided to go after the driver instead.

Jamming his revolver back in its holster, he reached for the door latch. Glorieta caught hold of his sleeve. "Custis, what are you doing?"

"Goin' up there to get the reins back from whoever's drivin' this coach to Mexico," Longarm replied. "Stay where you are and keep your head down."

"No! They'll kill you!"

They probably would when they got where they were going anyway, Longarm thought, but he didn't tell that to Glorieta. Instead he said, "Don't worry. I know what I'm doin'."

He hoped that was true.

Swinging the door open, he reached up and grabbed hold of the silver rail that ran around the top of the coach. As he leaned forward, his weight pulled him out the door. He caught the rail with his other hand and threw a leg up, getting his foot on the sill of the window. Muscles bunched in his arms, shoulders, and legs as he pulled himself upward. The wind of the coach's breakneck passage plucked his hat off and sent it spinning away through the air.

With a surge, Longarm sprawled on top of the racing vehicle. He turned his head toward the front of the coach and saw only one man on the box. That man wore a sombrero with its neck strap tight under his chin. The wide brim of the high-crowned hat was pushed up in the front. Salty was gone, no doubt clouted in the head and pitched off the coach back in Yuma when the current driver first jumped on. Longarm felt a flash of anger. If that old man wasn't all right . . .

First he had to deal with the threat of being kidnapped, then worry about what had happened to Salty. One of the riders veered closer to the coach and yelled something to the driver. The wind snatched away some of the Spanish words and the pounding of the team's hooves drowned out most of the others, but Longarm had a pretty good idea what the rider was shouting about. The fella was warning the driver that Longarm was on top of the coach.

The driver twisted on the seat and looked back. He shifted the reins to his left hand and used his right to claw at the pistol holstered on his hip. Unlike the riders who couldn't shoot toward the coach without the risk of a stray slug hitting Glorieta, the driver could blaze away at Longarm without worrying about that. And he fully intended to do so, from the looks of it. Longarm came up on hands and knees and threw himself forward as the driver's gun came around. Colt flame bloomed in the darkness, but the driver rushed his shot and it went wild. Longarm crashed against him, sledging a fist into the driver's jaw. Both men slid forward on the box.

For an instant, Longarm thought they were going to topple off the front of the box and fall under the slashing hooves of the team. But the kidnapper caught himself against the footboard, and Longarm grabbed hold of the silver rail at the end of the seat. The kidnapper kicked upward, aiming at Longarm's groin. Longarm twisted aside and grappled with the kidnapper. He didn't know where the reins had gone; probably they were trailing under the coach now. The horses were galloping as fast as ever, though. The stagecoach was a true runaway.

Longarm drove an elbow into the kidnapper's belly and then jabbed a punch into his face that bounced the man's head off the footboard. That stunned him. He stopped fighting. Longarm pushed himself up and reached for the brake lever, intending to stop the coach and try to hole up inside it with Glorieta until help arrived from Yuma. He had no idea how long that would be. He hoped someone had witnessed the kidnapping and would send the authorities after them.

His opponent recovered enough to grab him before he could reach the brake. The man's arm went around Longarm's neck from behind and jerked him backward. They scooted across the driver's box as the kidnapper tried to strangle him.

Though he had his hands a mite full trying to get free before he suffocated, Longarm noticed gun flashes in the darkness from one side of the coach. Were the kidnappers throwing caution to the winds and shooting at him? Or had pursuit from Yuma already caught up to them? He didn't know, and, at the moment, couldn't do anything about it either way. The arm across his throat was like a bar of iron, shutting off his air, and a red haze full of bright yellow sparks was starting to slide down over his vision, telling him that he was about to lose consciousness.

The coach hit some sort of bump just then and bounded high in the air, all four wheels coming off the ground. The jolt when it landed bounced Longarm and his opponent off the seat. Longarm realized to his horror that they were falling toward the horses again.

The kidnapper let go and tried to save himself. Falling facedown, Longarm threw his arms and legs out as far as they would go. His left arm and leg struck the back of one of the galloping horses. He grabbed on for dear life, digging his fingers into the animal's mane. He couldn't get any purchase with his leg, however, and he slid off to dangle for a second, supported only by the grip of one hand. Then his flailing right foot struck the thick wooden singletree to which the horses were hitched. He pushed himself up and got his other arm around the horse's neck.

Something hit his leg, which was braced against the singletree, almost dislodging it. Longarm gritted his teeth against the pain and twisted his head to look up and behind him. The kidnapper had caught his balance before falling off the box. Now the man was perched on the edge of the footboard, reaching over with one leg to kick at Longarm's leg. Longarm knew he couldn't hang on with just his arms. Another solid kick, two at most, would dislodge him and send him plummeting to his death under the hooves of the team.

He had to risk everything on a quick reach for his gun—assuming it hadn't fallen out of its holster while he was tussling with the kidnapper. Tightening his grip on the horse's neck with his left hand, Longarm let go with his right and sent it flashing across his body. His fingers closed around the butt of the Colt. The kidnapper got the same idea about then and grabbed for his own gun, abandoning his efforts to knock Longarm loose.

It was one of the trickiest shots Longarm had ever had to make. With his right arm between his body and the body of the horse, he pulled the Colt from its holster and angled the barrel up. He couldn't aim from this angle. Instinct had to guide his bullet. He fired just as the kidnapper cleared leather.

Traveling upward at a sharp angle, the slug ripped into the man's groin and bored through his body to burst out of his upper back. He screamed in pain and the gun in his hand blasted as his spasming finger involuntarily jerked the trigger. The bullet burned the rump of one of the horses and then plowed harmlessly into the ground. The kidnapper doubled over in agony as he lost consciousness and toppled forward off the coach.

For a terrible instant, Longarm thought the dying hombre was going to land on him and knock him loose from his perilous position. He dropped his gun and used both hands to cling to the horse once again as the kidnapper fell beside him, bounced off the singletree, and slid on underneath the pounding hooves. If he wasn't dead already, that finished him off. The coach lurched as the wheels ran over the body.

Longarm finally got both feet on the singletree. He shifted his grip to a more secure one holding the harness and was even able to reach down and gather up the loosely trailing reins. Bracing himself as securely as possible, he hauled back on the leathers and shouted, "Whoa! Whoa, damn it!"

The runaway horses slowed gradually. After a couple of minutes, Longarm was able to bring the coach to a bumping, swaying stop.

Now, unarmed, he had to deal with the rest of the kidnappers.

He had no idea what had happened during the past few minutes as he struggled desperately for his life. Now he turned and threw himself toward the driver's box, clambering onto it. Shots popped not far away, but he didn't know if they were directed at him. He dropped to the ground beside the coach and jerked open the door. "Glorieta!" he exclaimed. "Are you all right?"

She lifted her head and looked at him from where she lay huddled on the floor of the coach between the seats. "Oh, my God, Custis! I was afraid you were dead!"

He reached into the coach and grabbed her shoulders. "Are you hit?"

"N-no. I'm all right."

"Wouldn't happen to have a gun, would you?"

Glorieta reached over and twisted a latch Longarm hadn't seen before, opening a cabinet of sorts underneath the front seat. From it she pulled a sawed-off shotgun that she thrust into Longarm's hands. "Jerome keeps it there for emergencies!" she gasped.

Hearing hoofbeats pounding toward him, Longarm figured this qualified.

He spun around, using his elbow to knock the coach door shut as he turned. The onrushing rider was almost on top of him. A pistol barked, flame geysering from its muzzle. The bullet punched through the coach door over Longarm's head. Longarm lifted the scattergun and fired one barrel. A few of the buckshot peppered the horse and made it rear in pain, but most of the deadly charge tore into the rider and blew him out of the saddle.

Longarm heard the wind-rip of a bullet as another Colt-man closed in from the side. He turned and dropped to a knee, bringing the shotgun to his shoulder. The weapon roared deafeningly as he touched off the second barrel. Once again, the would-be kidnapper storming in on Longarm was thrown back by the impact of the buckshot slamming into him.

But the scattergun was empty now, and even if there were more shells in the hidden compartment under the coach seat, he didn't figure he'd have time to reload. He reversed the shotgun, gripping the twin barrels so that he could swing it as a short but dangerous club.

But to his surprise, the night seemed to be empty. The rest of the bunch that had stolen the stagecoach must have turned tail and run, he thought. He remembered the gun flashes he'd seen. Someone could have driven them off.

Sounds came out of the darkness. Hoofbeats again. But slower now, more deliberate. A voice called, "Hello the coach! Is everybody all right? Parker, where are you?"

Longarm hesitated. He recognized the voice. It belonged to the gambler named Tyler Branch. Had Branch followed them from Yuma to help them?

Or was he one of the kidnappers?

That seemed a little unlikely to Longarm, and the next moment his instinct was confirmed as Branch called out, "Those men who were after the coach took off for the tall and uncut. I'm coming in, so ease off the trigger."

Longarm opened the door of the coach and reached into the hidden compartment, feeling around until he found the box of shotgun shells he had hoped was there. "Stay low and keep quiet," he hissed to Glorieta as he broke open the scattergun, shucked the empties, and thumbed fresh shells into the barrels.

"All right," she whispered back.

Longarm turned toward Branch and eared back both hammers on the shotgun as the gambler rode slowly up to the coach. "That you, Parker?" Branch asked.

"It's me," Longarm admitted. "Keep your hands where I can see 'em, Branch."

"Hey, we're both on the same side, aren't we?" Branch sounded a little offended by Longarm's suspicion.

"Until I know what's what, I ain't on anybody's side but mine and Miss McCall's," Longarm grated.

Branch chuckled, evidently deciding that it would be easier to explain than to get angry. "I'm the one who traded shots with those men and ran them off," he said. "I saw what happened in Yuma."

"What did happen?" Longarm asked.

"Somebody jumped onto the driver's box of that coach from the second-floor gallery of a building it was passing. The fellow pistol-whipped the old man and pushed him off, then grabbed the reins and took off with the coach, driving hell-for-leather."

That matched up with what Longarm thought had happened. But Branch wasn't in the clear yet. "What did you do?"

"Ran over to see how bad the old-timer was hurt, of course. And I figured on raising the alarm and fetching the sheriff. But the old man told me that you and Miss McCall were inside the coach and were being kidnapped. When I saw that he was going to be all right, I told him to get the law while I came after you. I grabbed this horse and took off."

"Stole the horse, you mean?"

"Borrowed it," Branch said with another chuckle. "I'll see that it gets back to the proper owner. I don't think there'll be any trouble, since I was trying to stop a kid-napping."

The gambler was probably right about that.

"I was able to catch up with some hard riding," Branch went on. "Then I started shooting at the men who were riding around the coach. I'm a pretty fair pistol shot, if I do say so myself. I downed a couple of them and the rest took off, except for the two who were closest to the coach. It looks like you took care of them. Are they dead?"

"Wasn't time not to kill them," Longarm said. "Maybe the ones you shot are still alive, so the law can ask them some questions. Like who wants to kidnap Miss McCall."

He was pretty sure he already knew the answer to that, though.

More hoofbeats sounded as a large group of riders approached from the north. Longarm lifted the shotgun again. These newcomers weren't more kidnappers, however. Longarm heard Jerome Horton's worried voice raised in a shout. "Glorieta! Glorieta, where are you?"

By this time, Glorieta was climbing out of the stage-coach. Longarm looked over at her and said, "Why don't you let Horton know you're all right?"

She nodded. "Jerome!" She walked out a short distance from the coach, waving her arms over her head. "Jerome, we're over here!"

The riders galloped up with a dust cloud swirling in the moonlight behind them. Horton was out of the saddle before his horse even stopped moving, throwing his arms around Glorieta and hugging her tightly.

"Are you all right?" he asked in a choked voice. "Are you hurt?"

"I'm fine," she assured him. "Just shaken up a little."

Salty was with Horton, as were a spare, white-mustached man with a sheriff's star pinned on his coat and a dozen deputies and townsmen forming a makeshift posse. Longarm walked over to Salty and looked up at him. "I hear you got pistol-whipped. How bad were you hit?"

"Shoot, it weren't nothin'!" Salty insisted. "It'll take more'n a clout with a gun barrel to dent this ol' noggin o' mine. I see that young fella come after you like I told him to."

Longarm glanced at Tyler Branch and nodded. "That's right. He downed a couple of the outriders and ran off the others."

Horton turned to Branch. "Is that true, young man?"

Branch was still sitting on his horse. He shrugged. "I was just trying to lend a hand."

"I can't thank you enough." Horton looked over at Longarm. "Or you, Mr. Parker. Once again, I owe everything to you."

"We can talk about that later," Longarm said as he stowed the sawed-off shotgun in its compartment under the seat. "Right now, I reckon we'd better get back to Yuma and that riverboat, so that Miss McCall can rest."

"I'm fine," Glorieta insisted. "In fact, I found the whole experience to be quite . . . exhilarating . . ."

And with that, her eyes rolled up in her head and she fainted dead away.

Longarm was pretty sure that Glorieta would be all right. The excitement had just been too much for her. While she and Horton were taken back to Yuma in the stagecoach, now being driven again by Salty, Longarm and the sheriff checked the bodies of the men who had been killed in the kidnapping attempt. Unfortunately, they were all dead, so none of them would be answering any questions about who they were working for. Three of them were vaqueros; the other two were hard-faced Americans. Again, that supported the theory that they came from the Aragones *rancho* below the border.

"You know a young fella named Rafael Aragones?"

Longarm asked the sheriff. "His daddy, Don Hernando Aragones, has a big spread down in Sonora."

The elderly lawman shook his head. "Nope. I seem to remember seein' one o' them two gringos, though. Seem to recollect it was on a reward dodger."

"Wouldn't surprise me a bit. Things get a mite too hot for a Coltman on this side of the border, it's natural he'd drift down to mañana-land. Don Hernando's got some hard men working for him, from what I hear."

"You sound mighty positive these hombres ride for this Aragones fella, mister."

Longarm nodded. "I'm convinced of it."

And yet he had no proof, and he knew it. Longarm cautioned himself against jumping to conclusions. There could still be some other explanation for the attempts to kidnap Glorieta.

The posse started back toward Yuma. Longarm rode the horse that Salty had used earlier. Tyler Branch brought his mount alongside Longarm and commented, "I thought you were a goner when you fell off the driver's box on that coach."

Longarm grunted. "You and me, both, old son. Reckon I had a guardian angel in my back pocket lookin' out for me tonight."

"We can all use a little luck." Branch chuckled. "In my line of work, it's practically a necessity."

"Been gamblin' long?"

"A few years," Branch said offhandedly.

"And before that?"

"Before that I was an innocent child."

"You handle a gun pretty well," Longarm pointed out. "Those jaspers you shot were drilled plumb center."

"Unfortunately, violence sometimes dogs my profession. On occasion, poor losers like to console themselves by thinking that I cheated. They can believe that all they want, but when they give voice to it, trouble is inevitable."

Branch's tone hardened. "And for what it's worth, they're wrong. I don't cheat. Never have. I'm good enough so that I don't have to."

"I never said otherwise," Longarm pointed out.

Branch laughed softly. "Sorry. I guess that's just a sore point with me."

Longarm could understand. Most professional gamblers he had run across *were* cheats. But there was a handful who weren't, and they prided themselves on their ability to make a living with the pasteboards without having to resort to trickery and connivance. Longarm supposed it was something like the way honest lawmen felt about the ones who were crooked. Star packers who walked the straight and narrow despised any lawman who bent the law instead of upholding it.

When they got back to Yuma, Longarm and Branch rode straight to the riverboat landing while the sheriff returned to his office and the rest of the posse scattered. The undertaker would go out with his wagon come morning to gather up the corpses.

Salty was waiting at the landing. "I'll take them hosses back to where they belong," he offered.

"You sure you're all right?" Longarm asked. "I've had a few gun barrels bent over my head, and it's an experience that don't leave a fella feeling any too spry."

"I'm fine," Salty insisted. "Now gimme them reins."

Longarm and Branch handed over the horses, and the old man led them up the street toward the livery barn. Salty's mount had come from there, and it was likely the liveryman would know who owned the horse Branch had "borrowed."

"I don't know about you," Branch said as he and Longarm walked across the gangplank to the deck of the *Manatee*, "but after everything that's happened I could use a drink."

That sounded like a good idea to Longarm. "You

wouldn't happen to know if they have any Maryland rye in that salon, would you?"

"As a matter of fact, they do. Tom Moore. I drink it myself."

Longarm grinned. "I could tell by lookin' that you were a man of sophisticated tastes, Mr. Branch."

"Shall we adjourn to the salon, then, Mr. Parker?"

Longarm ran a thumbnail along his jawline. "I'll be there in a few minutes. I want to go to my cabin and sluice some o' this dust off, maybe put on a clean shirt."

"All right," Branch nodded. "I'll see you shortly."

He strolled toward the front of the boat. Longarm went to the door of his cabin, but before he could go inside, the door of the cabin next to his opened and Jerome Horton stepped out on deck, closing the door quietly behind him.

"I've been waiting for you to get back, Mr. Parker," Horton said. "I take it there was no more trouble."

"Not a bit," Longarm said with a shake of his head. "The rest of that bunch was long gone. After losing five men, there wasn't any fight left in them."

"They were Aragones's men?"

"Nobody knows for sure. Seems likely, though." Longarm paused, then asked, "How's Miss McCall?"

"She's fine. Or at least she will be after a good night's rest. I had the local doctor look at her, and he said she's just suffering from the strain of being in such danger. She's sleeping now. I'll watch over her."

"I don't reckon you'll have any more trouble tonight, but I won't be far off, just in case. I'm going to clean up a mite, then have a drink in the salon with Tyler Branch."

"Oh, yes, that young fellow." Horton sounded vaguely disapproving of Branch, but that was because he was jealous, Longarm knew.

"Branch came in mighty handy tonight," Longarm pointed out. "Without his help, I might not have been able to get Miss McCall away from those hombres."

"I'll have to be sure to thank him, then," Horton said stiffly. "Please inform the bartender in the salon that Mr. Branch's drinks are on the house tonight. And yours as well, of course."

"Much obliged. I hear there's Maryland rye in there."

"Only the best," Horton said with a smile.

He went back in the cabin, again closing the door quietly so as not to disturb Glorieta's rest. Longarm went next door, washed up with the water in a basin on the small table next to the bed, and put on a clean shirt.

The salon was on the third deck and was large enough to take up nearly half the space. Longarm walked up the steps between decks and turned to go through a pair of double doors into the big room. It reminded him of a barroom in a fine hotel, with a polished hardwood bar, cut-glass chandeliers, and poker tables scattered around. There was even a roulette wheel, though no one was using it at the moment.

The *Manatee*'s passenger list included mining executives, salesmen, ranchers, and even a few prospectors who had scraped up the price of a ticket and were treating themselves to a ride up the river before returning to their hardscrabble existence in the Arizona badlands. Several men were drinking at the bar, including Tyler Branch. A couple of poker games were going on at the tables. Longarm had a feeling Branch would be joining one of them pretty soon.

The bar was on the other side of the salon. Longarm started across the room toward it. His path took him past a table where a woman sat, dealing a hand of solitaire. Her back was to him, but he admired the thick auburn hair that fell to smooth white shoulders left bare by her dark green gown. She was the only woman in the room, Longarm noted.

He had just walked behind her when he heard her say

softly, "Oh, my God." Thinking something was wrong, he stopped and turned around. He was startled to see that she was staring up at him, as if he were the one who had prompted her exclamation.

She was just as pretty from the front as from the back. Though no longer young, she had settled into that classic, gracious beauty that some women are lucky enough to possess when they grow older. Not that she was *old*, Longarm thought. She was a couple of years younger than he was, at most. Her figure was still firm and attractive, as demonstrated by the low-cut gown that showed off the upper halves of her creamy breasts. The thing that sent a shock through him, though, was the way she was looking at him, as if she knew him.

She did know him. She proved that by saying, "I thought that looked like you from the back, but I wasn't sure. But how could I ever forget those shoulders? They haven't changed." She came to feet. "Custis, it *is* you. My God, after all these years, and in this place . . ." She reached out to him. "I can't believe it. Custis Long, in the flesh!"

Chapter 8

Well, now, this was a problem, Longarm thought as he instinctively took the hands the woman held out to him. Folks around these parts knew him as Custis Parker, a drifting gunman working for Jerome Horton as a bodyguard to the world famous Arizona Flame, and here was this woman announcing to the world that his name was really Custis Long. Did she know that he was a deputy U.S. marshal, too?

And for that matter, who the hell was she? Longarm thought she looked a mite familiar, but he couldn't place her.

She must have seen the confusion on his face. "Don't you know me, Custis?" she asked as she squeezed his hands. "It's Estelle. Estelle Henry." She leaned closer and lowered her voice so that only he could hear what she said. "But I'll bet you remember me as Stella Jean Harwell."

Longarm's eyes widened. *Good Lord*, he thought. *Stella Jean Harwell*. He remembered her, all right.

The last time he'd seen her, they had both been naked as jaybirds, and she'd been straddling his hips with his shaft deep inside her, gasping in passion as her hips pumped back and forth and she rode him like there was no tomorrow.

Twenty years ago. No, more than that, Longarm thought. Closer to twenty-five. Before the war.

"Stella Jean?" he said hoarsely.

She stepped closer to him, slipped her hands out of his, and threw her arms around his neck. Her body molded to his as she hugged him tightly.

Yep, Longarm thought. Same old Stella Jean.

It was West-by-God-Virginia, a place filled with rugged mountains and deep, dark valleys. He had been little more than a boy, a man-child near fully grown, and Stella Jean Harwell was a pretty girl with long hair the color of autumn leaves and the misfortune to live on a farm with a drunken, dirt-poor father, a slatternly mother, and a double handful of siblings who were about as dumb as a bag of rocks. Stella Jean was the only one of the family who was worth anything at all. Custis Long felt sorry for her and let her tag along when he went fishing, and one day down by the creek, when nothing was biting, she peeled off her ragged cotton dress—the only garment she wore—and pulled down his britches so that she could have her way with him. Young Custis didn't put up too much of an argument when she tugged him on top of her, grasped his shaft in her eager hand, and tucked him away inside her. It wasn't the first time for either of them, but it was the best so far, at least for Longarm.

After that, they had done it every chance they got, wherever they happened to be. Stella Jean didn't say anything about a preacher or even hint that she wanted to marry up with him. She had the appetites of youth and a sheer love for what she was doing. Custis Long figured he was just about the luckiest young fella on the face of the earth. Their affair went on for several months.

Then Stella Jean's father, drunk as a skunk as usual,

fell down while he was working in one of the family's fields, cut his arm open on the plow, and lay there and bled to death because he was sunk too deep in a drunken stupor to get up or even to yell for help. Stella Jean's mother had taken all the kids and moved off to Kentucky, where she had kinfolks. Stella Jean promised that she would run away and come back to young Custis, and she'd made love with him one last time to seal the bargain.

But she hadn't come back, and then the war had started and Longarm had gone off to fight. After it was over and he'd seen too much to ever return to the life of a farmer, he had headed West . . .

And here he was, all those years later, never having seen Stella Jean Harwell again. She had faded in his memory until he couldn't even call up an image of her in his mind. He still thought fondly of her, every now and then, but not often.

Life sure had a way of playing tricks on a fella.

She leaned back in his embrace and looked up at him. "What is it, Custis?" she asked. "What's wrong? You *do* remember me, don't you?"

"Sure, I remember you, Stella Jean," he said huskily.

"Estelle. I go by Estelle now."

"Yeah. Estelle Henry. Your married name?"

She laughed softly. "The name of the husband I liked the best. I've been married three times. And widowed three times, may they rest in peace. But none of them could ever measure up to you, Custis." A suggestive gleam came into her eyes. "Not in any way."

Longarm swallowed. "Well, it's, uh, mighty good to see you again . . ."

"No, you don't," Estelle said firmly. "Don't you even think about running off. After all these years, I'm not just about to let you go that easily. We have a lot of catching up to do."

Someone cleared his throat behind Longarm. Tyler Branch said, "I see you two know each other."

Longarm looked around to see Branch standing there, a drink in his hand and an amused smile on his face.

"Know each other?" Estelle repeated. "Of course we know each other! Custis and I go way back, don't we, Custis?"

"I reckon so." She hadn't used his full name yet where Branch could hear it, he thought. Maybe he could steer her back to the table before she said anything else.

"Why don't we have a drink?" he suggested, taking her arm.

"That sounds like a wonderful idea. Tyler, you join us."

Longarm's heart sank. Clearly, Estelle and Branch were acquainted. He didn't see any way out of this.

"I'd be glad to," Branch said. "Mr. Parker and I were supposed to have a drink together anyway, and I never object to your lovely presence, Estelle."

At the mention of the name "Parker," Estelle's eyes flicked toward Longarm. Would she remember that was his middle name? Would she figure out that he was using it on purpose and didn't want his real identity revealed? She had always been quick-witted, back in the days when she'd been Stella Jean. Longarm hoped that as Estelle, she was just as fast on the uptake.

She smiled and started gathering up the cards she'd laid out on the table. "You two gentlemen sit down right here," she said. "What are you drinking, Mr. Parker?"

Longarm forced himself not to heave a sigh of relief. That was her way of letting him know that she understood the situation, he thought. "Maryland rye," he said.

"There's a bottle of Tom Moore under the bar," Branch put in. "Why don't you bring the whole thing over here, Estelle?"

"Of course." She moved toward the bar with a swish of skirts and petticoats.

Longarm and Branch sat down at the table. "So you've known Estelle for a long time?" Branch said.

"Quite a while," Longarm replied. "How about you?"

"Only a couple of years. But I'm quite fond of her. She taught me nearly everything I know about cards."

Longarm's eyebrows lifted slightly in surprise. "She's a gambler, too?"

"One of the best. She worked the riverboats on the Mississippi for years, she told me, before coming West. She's been in California recently. I met her in San Francisco. I didn't know she was going to be on this boat until I boarded earlier today and ran into her." Branch smiled fondly toward the bar, where Estelle was picking up a silver tray with the bottle of rye and two glasses on it. Branch already had a glass. He sipped from it as Estelle came back over to the table.

"You two seem to know each other as well," she said as she sat down and poured drinks for herself and Longarm. "Have you been acquainted long?"

"We just met earlier today," Branch said. "But we've shared a lot since then, haven't we, Mr. Parker?"

"I reckon you could say that." Longarm looked at Estelle and explained, "This young fella gave me a hand earlier tonight when there was some trouble."

"Trouble? What sort of trouble?"

"Have you heard of the Arizona Flame?" Branch asked.

"That girl who was supposed to sing at the Opera House? I heard some talk about it. She's Jerome Horton's mistress, isn't she?"

Longarm shook his head in response to the blunt question. "She's a singer, all right, but Mr. Horton looks on her like a daughter. He's just interested in gettin' her singing career started right."

Estelle looked at him with a skeptical expression on her

lovely face. "Honey, don't you know that no man thinks of a pretty girl as his daughter unless she actually is? Horton's interested in her, you can take my word for that, and I don't even know the girl. But how's she tied in with this trouble you mentioned?"

"Somebody tried to kidnap her," Longarm said. "And me, too, since I was with her at the time. I'm workin' for Horton, lookin' out for the girl."

"Really?" Estelle arched her eyebrows. "You're a gunman for hire these days, Custis?"

"I do what I can to make my way," Longarm replied uneasily, not knowing whether Estelle was aware of his real profession or not. She seemed to be willing to play along with whatever he said, though. And if his true identity came out, it wouldn't be a catastrophe, he told himself. It might make his job of finding the bullion thieves a little harder, but so far he hadn't had much luck anyway.

Estelle looked over at Branch. "And what's your part in this, Tyler?"

"I happened to see what was going on and pitched in to lend a hand."

"Gunplay again?" Estelle asked, disapprovingly. She sounded a little like a mother chiding a wayward son.

Branch shrugged and gave her a grin. "It seemed like the thing to do at the time, since the kidnappers were shooting at me."

"But neither one of you was hurt?"

Longarm shook his head, and so did Branch. "Neither was the girl," Longarm said. "We were all mighty lucky."

Estelle lifted her glass. "We should drink to Lady Luck, then, since she seems to be smiling on you tonight. On all of us," she added, "since I consider myself lucky to have run into you again, Custis."

"I'll drink to that," Longarm murmured. The three glasses clinked together above the center of the table.

For the next half hour, they sat there drinking and talking. Longarm kept the references to the past vague, and Estelle went along with that. She suggested that they play some poker, but Longarm shook his head.

"It's been a long day," he said. "I might ought to turn in. I ain't as young as I used to be."

Estelle laughed. "Don't say that, Custis. If you're not as young as you used to be, then I can't be, either."

"You don't have to worry about that. You're more beautiful now than you were back home—and you were the prettiest gal in the whole state then."

"My, aren't you the gallant one!" Estelle smiled at Branch. "You could learn some things from this one, Tyler."

"Yes, I imagine I could," Branch said with a faint smile of his own.

Longarm stood up and bent over to kiss Estelle on the cheek. "I'll be on the boat all the way to Hardyville," he said. "I reckon we'll run into each other again."

"I'm sure we will," Estelle said. "Good night, Custis."

"Good night."

He gave Branch a casual wave and left the salon, but as he reached the desk outside, he paused and rasped his thumbnail along his jawline. He'd have given a pretty penny to know what those two were saying to each other now that he was gone. He supposed he trusted Estelle; even if she knew his secret, she had no reason to betray him. And if she didn't know he was a lawman, she probably thought he was using a different name because of some past scrape.

Longarm gave a little shake of his head and went to his cabin. Fretting over things never changed them. It was just a waste of energy.

He dropped his hat on the table next to the bed, took off his gunbelt and coiled it next to the hat. He sat down on the bed to pull off his boots, then peeled off his shirt and draped it over the back of the cabin's only chair. He was about to unfasten his pants when a soft knock came on the door.

Glorieta? he thought. Had she awakened and found Horton asleep, then decided to slip over here to continue what they had started in the coach before the kidnapping. Or was it someone else?

He drew his gun and padded over to the door. "Who is it?"

"Estelle."

That didn't come as a surprise. Longarm threw the latch and opened the door. Estelle stood there on the deck with a lacy shawl wrapped around her bare shoulders. She had a bottle of rye in one hand and two glasses in the other. Longarm couldn't tell if it was the same bottle of Tom Moore or not.

"Don't you invite a lady in when she comes calling, Custis?" Estelle asked with a smile. She looked down at the gun in his hand. "Or were you expecting some other sort of company?"

Longarm stepped back. "Come on in." He closed the door behind her, then went over to the table and slid the Colt back in its holster. "I reckon I'm in the habit of being careful."

"That's a good habit to be in, for a man in your line of work."

Was she just teasing him? Did she know he was really a star packer?

"I suppose a bodyguard has to be careful all the time," she said.

Longarm shrugged.

"And a man who uses a different name than the one he grew up with is usually no stranger to trouble."

"Parker *is* my name," Longarm said. "Custis Parker Long."

"I remember. And I'm not asking any questions. What you call yourself, what you do for a living, those things

110

are your business, Custis, and none of mine." She stepped closer to him, so that he could smell the perfume she wore. "I remember this broad, hairy chest of yours, too. You were always . . . well built." Her eyes dropped suggestively to his groin.

Longarm felt a stirring inside him. Not only was Estelle Henry a very attractive woman in her own right, but the history they shared together, the memories they had in common, added some extra spice to the delicious tension that existed between them. They had known every square inch of each other's body, had explored those bodies with fingers and lips and tongues. The passage of years had changed them some, of course, but the years had been extremely kind to Estelle. And Longarm's rugged life had kept age from softening him. They were both still in their prime, and as Longarm looked at her, he felt the aches and pains and weariness of the day vanishing as passion began to burn inside him.

The same heat was in Estelle's eyes. She set the bottle and the glasses on the table and said, "I don't think we need these right now, do we?"

"Maybe later," Longarm said. He reached for her, and she came willingly, eagerly, into his arms.

The hot, sweet taste of her mouth instantly transported him back to his youth. But as Estelle's tongue slid into his mouth, Longarm realized he was wrong to be dwelling on the past. Stella Jean Harwell had been a girl—a sensuous, exciting, downright lusty girl, to be sure—but Estelle Henry was a *woman*. She was every bit as sensuous and exciting and lusty as her younger self had been, but now she had years of experience to go with those other sterling qualities.

And she had acquired patience, too. Rather than getting them both naked as fast as possible and then jumping on him, as she had done in the past, tonight she seemed content to take it slow and easy. So was Longarm. He held

111

her and kissed her for long, tantalizing moments, moving his head back and forth and brushing his lips over hers, flicking his tongue against her mouth. Her tongue met his, and they circled warily, wetly, in a slick, darting dance. Longarm slid his hands up from her waist to her bare shoulders, stroking her skin with his fingertips, working his touch in along her throat. His right hand cupped her chin while his left stole behind her neck, under the cascade of thick, auburn hair. He held her gently, almost like she was a butterfly nestled in the palms of his hands.

When he finally broke the kiss, he moved his lips to the hollow of her throat and then lowered his head slowly until he was kissing the top of the valley between her breasts. She sighed and leaned against him. He tugged a little on the bodice of her gown, and it slipped down, baring her full breasts. Estelle closed her eyes and pressed on the sides of the fleshy globes, surrounding Longarm's face with soft woman flesh.

He kissed and licked her breasts for several minutes, then moved his lips to the nipple of the left one. He sucked the hard brown nubbin into his mouth and ran his tongue around it. After laving that nipple for several minutes, he switched to the other one. Estelle ran her fingers through his hair as he continued his oral caresses.

Lowering her bodice to get at her breasts was one thing; divesting her of the gown, assorted petticoats, and other undergarments was another, and considerably more complicated. Luckily, Longarm had quite a bit of experience at undressing ladies. Eventually, he was able to get her shed of most of her clothes. She wound up wearing nothing but stockings and garters. Longarm dropped to his knees in front of her and stroked the silky hair that covered the mound at the juncture of her thighs. Estelle parted her legs a little so that he could slip his hand between them. His fingers found and toyed with the folds of her sex. They were slick with her juices already, so it was

112

easy for him to slip a finger inside her. "Oh, Custis," she said as he penetrated her. He added a second finger to the first one, and she gave a pleasured gasp.

Longarm slipped his fingers in and out of her. She grew even wetter. Keeping his fingers inside her, he leaned closer and used his tongue to tease the little bud of flesh at the top of her slit. Her hips jerked, and she pushed her pelvis against his face.

After a moment, she managed to say, "This . . . this isn't . . . fair!"

"You want me to stop?" Longarm asked.

"That's not what I . . . meant. Oh! I want to . . . give you some pleasure . . . Custis." She tugged at his shoulders. "Come on. Lie back on the bed . . ."

Since space was always at a premium on a boat, the bed was narrow, little more than a bunk. But the mattress on it was comfortable, and Longarm felt his muscles easing as he stretched out. Estelle knelt beside the bed and lowered her head over his groin. She wrapped both hands around the long, thick pole that jutted up from the thick nest of hair. She began to lick his shaft, starting at the base, just above the heavy sacs, and working her way toward the crown. When she had tasted every bit of it, she opened her lips wide and took the head into her mouth.

She held his manhood steady with one hand while she sucked it and used the other hand to cup his balls and gently roll them back and forth. Her little finger strayed lower still to tickle the sensitive flesh she found there. Deep in his chest, Longarm made a rumbling sound of pure pleasure, like the purr of a massive lion.

Estelle continued the French lesson for a long time, and Longarm loved every minute of it. Finally, she lifted her head and moved languidly, sinuously, above him. "I always did like to be on top," she whispered. "Is that all right, Custis?"

Longarm could barely talk. "Only a crazy man would say it wasn't," he croaked. "And I ain't completely lost my wits yet."

She wasn't through teasing him, though. First she lay down on top of him and slid her body back and forth on his. Her breasts flattened against his chest. She was straddling him, so each time she moved back, his organ brushed up against her soaked, inviting opening. But she slid forward again before he could penetrate her, so all he felt was a promise of heat. She rained kisses down on his face and chest and tugged at his nipples. With each caress, another throb of need went through his shaft.

Two could play at that game. Longarm reached behind her to cup the cheeks of her rump. He kneaded and squeezed the soft flesh and used his middle finger to explore the valley between the mounds. Estelle was breathing hard now. She caught her bottom lip between her teeth for a moment. When she let it go, she panted, "I don't know how much longer . . . I can wait . . . Custis."

"I'm ready if . . . you are."

"Oh, yes. I'm ready."

She proved it by resting her hands against his chest and sitting up, poising herself over his manhood. She lowered herself onto the shaft, her femininity opening and spreading around the thick pole, gradually engulfing it as she sank lower and lower. "Oh, my!" she exclaimed as Longarm's organ filled her. "Has it . . . has it grown since I saw you last, Custis?"

"You bring out the best in me, darlin'," he told her with a smile.

At last he was sheathed fully inside her. He cupped her breasts and used his thumbs to play with her nipples as her hips began thrusting and rotating. Longarm met each of her movements with strokes of his own. In and out his shaft drove. "Deeper! Deeper!" she chanted, and he

114

wanted to give her what she asked for. But it was impossible, because he was as deep inside her as he could go. The head of his shaft was butting up against her very core.

The leisurely pace at which they had begun was abandoned by common consent. She was humping the hell out of him by now, and he was giving it right back to her. Just like the old days, their passions had enflamed them until they were out of control. Longarm wasn't even thinking now. He had become a creature of pure instinct, pure need, pure desire.

And when his climax seized him, it was with the shattering ferocity of a desert thunderstorm, pouring out of him in a white hot flood that sent Estelle spiraling over the edge into her own culmination. He gripped her hips and arched his back and reached so far inside her to empty himself that it seemed they were two parts of one whole, no longer separate entities at all.

It was good, damned good.

When it was over, Longarm fell back on the bed and Estelle collapsed on top of him. He was about half senseless and figured she was, too. He held her and kissed the top of her head as she rested it on his chest.

"Custis," she said breathlessly, "you're still the best . . . I ever had."

"I'm much obliged you think so."

She lifted her head to look at him. "You're going all the way upriver, you said?"

"That's right."

"Good. Because before we get to Hardyville, I plan to plumb wear you out, mister."

Longarm laughed, because that sounded just like something Stella Jean Harwell would have said. He supposed you could take the girl out of West-by-God Virginia, but you couldn't take the West-by-God Virginia out of the girl.

Chapter 9

The Colorado was not the prettiest river in the world as it passed through southwestern Arizona Territory, nor was the landscape itself all that attractive. The river wound between steep, rust-colored bluffs backed up by rugged, mostly rocky hills and small mountains. The blue of the river and the sky were the only bright colors. Everything else was painted in hues of brown and tan and ocher. Still, the terrain did have a certain stark beauty to it, Longarm thought as he stood on the deck of the *Manatee* with his hands resting on the railing. The problem was that it got old in a hurry.

Jerome Horton and Glorieta McCall were strolling along the deck a few feet away. Longarm was keeping an eye on them, even though it was highly unlikely there would be any trouble while the riverboat was chugging upstream like this, the great paddle wheel at its stern revolving rapidly and throwing a spray of water into the air all around it. The only way kidnappers could strike at Glorieta while the boat was moving would be to try to stop the vessel somehow and take her off of it. It was much more likely they would attempt to grab her while the *Manatee* was stopped at Ehrenberg.

The riverboat had left Yuma at dawn. Tuckered out from the events of the day before and the night's enthusiastic lovemaking with Estelle, Longarm had slept through the departure, even though Captain O'Brien had blown the whistle several times and the boat's boilers were thumping loudly belowdecks. Longarm had arisen later, had a leisurely breakfast in the salon, which doubled as the dining room, and then joined Horton and Glorieta in their promenade along the deck. So far this morning, Longarm hadn't seen any sign of Estelle or Tyler Branch. They were probably sleeping in, since gamblers tended to be nocturnal folks and were seldom seen out of bed before the middle of the day.

A footstep sounded behind Longarm. "Mornin'," Salty said.

Longarm turned to grin at the old-timer. "I didn't know if you were coming upriver with us or not. Thought you might stay in Yuma with the stagecoach."

Salty shook his head as he stepped up to the railing. "Nope, I decided to come along. Mr. Horton didn't mind. The coach'll be fine there in the company's barn in Yuma. I ain't rid on a riverboat in years. Thought it might be a nice change."

"Well, I'm glad to have you along for the ride," Longarm said, meaning it. He liked Salty, and the old man might be handy to have around in case of trouble. He had proven during the chase after the bullion thieves south of Casa Grande that he could handle himself in a fight.

Longarm checked to see that Horton and Glorieta were still strolling along the deck, then he leaned his forearms on the rail and said, "I reckon Horton's still mixin' business with pleasure on this part of the trip."

Salty frowned. "What do you mean by that? I told you, he ain't foolin' around with that girl—"

Longarm raised a hand to forestall Salty's protest. "That's not what I was gettin' at. I'm talking about his

118

bullion-totin' business. This boat of his is going to be stopping in Ehrenberg, La Paz, and Hardyville. That's its regular run. Don't the mines around those places ship out their bullion on the boat?"

"I reckon they do," Salty admitted. "We'll be takin' on shipments of gold and silver to carry back downriver to Yuma. From there, the bullion'll be loaded on wagons and freighted to Tucson to be put on the railroad there." Salty gave Longarm a shrewd look. "You know, if you hadn't gone after that bunch o' thieves with the posse and nearly got your head shot off along with the rest of us, questions like that'd make me figure you might be part o' the gang."

"But you know I'm not," Longarm said.

"Like I said, you went after 'em." Salty shrugged. "I like to think I'm a pretty good judge o' character, too, and you don't strike me as the owlhoot type. A gunman, sure, but not a cold-blooded killer or a bullion thief."

"Well, I'm obliged for that," Longarm said with a grin. He grew more serious as he went on, "Seems to me like that bunch will try to hit us again somewhere on this trip, if they follow the same pattern. I'd like to outguess 'em and maybe be waiting for them when they jump us."

"That don't have anything to do with guardin' the gal, and that's your job, ain't it?"

"If there's trouble, she could wind up in danger," Longarm pointed out.

Salty snorted. "If you ask me, that ain't it at all. You're just a natural-born trouble-hunter, Custis. Some fellas just ain't happy if they have to go too long without the smell o' gunsmoke in their nose."

"You've got me all wrong, Salty. I'm a peaceable man."

Salty just snorted again in disbelief as the *Manatee* paddled on upriver.

· · ·

Ehrenberg was called Mineral City when it was founded, an apt name considering all the mines located in the area. Later, the name had been changed to honor Hermann Ehrenberg, one of the local pioneers. The town was set on the west bank of the river, in a spot where a good number of willows grew. Trees of any sort were unusual in this mostly arid landscape, so Ehrenberg was a spot of shady relief from the constant sun and heat. The adobe structures of the original settlement had been augmented by quite a few log and frame buildings, including the River View Hotel, one of the nicest hostelries in the entire territory. The wharves at the riverboat landing were sturdy and extended a good distance into the water. Ehrenberg was a bustling frontier town, full of everything that made the West so exciting and so hazardous at the same time.

Longarm stood near the bow of the boat with Horton and Glorieta as it approached the landing, two and a half days after leaving Yuma. Captain Henry O'Brien was with them. The captain said proudly, "We've made good time, if I do say so myself. I don't expect to maintain that pace for the entire voyage, however. I've yet to see a time when we weren't slowed down at least a little by low water farther upstream."

"That exposes all the sandbars, doesn't it?" Longarm asked. He had traveled on enough riverboats in his life to be aware of the problems that could plague them.

O'Brien nodded. "Low water in itself will cause us to slow down, but when the sandbars are out, it's even worse. They shift about in the riverbed, you know, so one isn't sure from one trip to the next exactly where they're located."

"But we'll be able to avoid them, won't we, Captain?" Glorieta asked.

"I'll do my best, ma'am," O'Brien assured her. "I have a pair of excellent pilots, and one of them is always up there in the pilothouse, directing the helmsman. With all due modesty, I must say that I'm an adequate pilot myself, if the need arises for me to fill that role."

Curious, Longarm asked, "What's the fastest you ever made this run?"

"From Yuma to Hardyville—ten days." O'Brien smiled. "Don't expect that this time, however. We've had good depth to the river, but there haven't been enough rains in recent months to keep it that way farther upstream. The level will drop consistently from here on. At times, it's taken almost two months to make the voyage to Hardyville. Don't expect that, either. The weather hasn't been *that* dry."

Hearing voices, Longarm looked back along the railing and saw Estelle Henry and Tyler Branch walking toward the bow, arm-in-arm. They were talking and laughing. Longarm knew that a friendship existed between the two of them, so he didn't feel jealous. He and Estelle had made love several times since leaving Yuma, and he was pretty sure that there was nothing romantic between her and Branch, just a kinship born of the fact that both of them made their livings with cards.

"Good morning," Estelle said brightly as she and Branch came up to the group at the bow. It was actually early afternoon, but no one corrected her. "That's Ehrenberg up ahead, isn't it?" The town was visible, no more than half a mile upriver.

"That is correct, Mrs. Henry," O'Brien said, touching two fingers to the brim of his cap. "I trust you're enjoying the voyage so far?"

"Oh, very much so." Estelle looked at Longarm and smiled. "It's been one of the best trips I've ever taken."

From the corner of his eye, Longarm saw the frown that appeared on Glorieta's face as Estelle spoke. He didn't know if Glorieta was aware of what was going on between him and Estelle, or if she just felt a natural dislike for the older woman. Glorieta had to be aware, though, that she hadn't been able to spend any time alone with Longarm since the boat left Yuma, and it seemed like that was bothering her.

Longarm was sorry about that, but he was thoroughly enjoying his reunion with Estelle. Not only was it wonderful to be able to bed her again and delight in all her physical charms, but also they had spent hours talking about the days when they had both been young. Longarm had never been one to waste time looking back; what was ahead of him was much more interesting, as far as he was concerned. But it was nice on occasion to remember how things had been when he was younger, the good times and the bad, and all the people he had known during those days. He was glad he had run into Estelle. He wouldn't have missed what he had with her for the world.

Now she moved up beside him at the rail and asked, "Have you been to Ehrenberg before, Custis?"

"Several times," Longarm replied. "Not for a good while, though. From here, it doesn't look like it's changed much."

Branch commented, "I hear that the Mineral City Saloon and Music Hall is quite a place."

Longarm nodded. The establishment Branch had mentioned was the largest saloon in town and had gotten its name from the original settlement. In addition to being a saloon, it was a theater of sorts as well. Glorieta would be performing there. The date of her appearance had been left flexible, since her arrival depended on the river and how quickly the *Manatee* could cover the distance from Yuma up here.

"I know McDermott will be glad to see us," Horton said, referring to the owner of the Mineral City. "He expects that the Music Hall will be packed."

Glorieta just smiled. She was losing some of her nervousness and gaining confidence as the trip went on, Longarm thought. The performances in Casa Grande, Gila

Bend, and Yuma had all gone very well, so Glorieta knew that she would have no trouble winning over the audience. The kidnapping attempts had come after the shows and had had nothing to do with them.

O'Brien tugged on the brim of his cap and said, "If you ladies and gentlemen will excuse me, I ought to go up to the pilothouse while we're coming in to the landing."

He left to climb the ladders to the pilothouse, perched as high atop the riverboat as it could get. The others stood at the railing and watched as the *Manatee* was maneuvered deftly alongside one of the docks. Once the boat had been tied up, deckhands began unloading the cargo that had been brought upriver. Most of it was crates of merchandise bound for Ehrenberg's several emporiums and general stores. There was also some mining equipment in larger, heavier crates.

Once again, the travelers would be spending the night on board, even though the River View was an excellent hotel. Horton had decided it would be more trouble than it was worth to move all of his and Glorieta's things to the hotel for just one night. Longarm didn't mind. He wanted to stick pretty close to the boat anyway, since it was possible some gold or silver bullion would be brought aboard. He toyed with the idea of telling Horton who he really was, so that he could ask the man directly what the plans were, but he decided to hold off just a little longer and see what happened.

There was still Don Rafael Aragones to worry about, too. Longarm felt that it would be harder for Aragones's men to get to Glorieta on the boat than it would be if she were to spend the night in the hotel.

Estelle would be spending the night on shore, though, as she explained to Longarm a short time after the *Manatee* docked, while they were in her cabin. "From what I've heard, there's always at least one high-stakes game going on in the back room of the Mineral City. I've been neglecting my work during this trip, Custis, and it's all your fault." She gave him a mock pout. "I've been too busy romping with you to play poker."

"I'm sorry about that, I reckon," he said, his voice a little strangled because of what she'd been doing to him for the past few minutes. "Then again, maybe I ain't."

She gave him a mischievous grin and took his manhood back in her mouth. He was sitting on the edge of her bed with his trousers and long underwear pulled down, while she knelt in front of him fully dressed. Her head bobbed up and down a little as she sucked on him. Gradually, she worked her way lower until she had swallowed almost half of his shaft. That was better than most gals could manage. Longarm watched in awe as Estelle took in still more of his organ. Her tongue swirled and swooped around it until he couldn't stand the sweet torment any longer. "Hang on," he warned Estelle as a huge throb went through his shaft and his seed began to burst from the opening at the end.

She kept her lips clamped tightly to him as the muscles in her throat worked and she swallowed every drop of the climax that poured out of him. Longarm emptied himself into her mouth.

"I'm going to miss you tonight, Custis," she said as she stood up and sat next to him on the bed for a moment. "A girl's got to make a living, though."

"We'll have more chances to get together on the way upriver," he assured her. "It's a long way yet to Hardy-ville."

Later that afternoon, he accompanied Horton and Glorieta to the Mineral City Saloon and Music Hall, where he met Angus McDermott, the Scotsman who owned and ran the place. Instead of the slender, dour Scot Longarm had been expecting, McDermott turned out to be short, rotund, and jolly, with a perpetual grin. He greeted them effusively and then took Glorieta's arm, practically dragging her through an arched entrance into the music hall part of the establishment, where she would be performing in a few hours. "Ye'll want t' take a good look at th' place," McDermott told her, "so ye'll know wha' t' expect when ye come oot this evenin'."

Longarm leaned an elbow against the jamb of the entrance and watched as Glorieta took a turn around the stage with Horton and McDermott. He glanced over his shoulder and saw Estelle settling in at one of the poker tables. Tyler Branch was at a different table. Obviously, they didn't want to play against each other. That would just cut down on the winnings for one of them. This way, they could forget about their fondness for each other and concentrate on separating the other players from their *dinero*.

Horton and Glorieta had supper in a private dining room with McDermott. Longarm made a meal from the free lunch counter in the Mineral City's barroom, along with Salty, who had drifted in late in the afternoon. " 'Tain't much to see in Ehrenberg," the old man said, "but I seen what there was of it."

McDermott had posters announcing Glorieta's performance all printed up and ready. As soon as he'd gotten word that the riverboat had docked, he'd sent boys out all over town to tack up the posters. The news spread fast. By early evening, men were coming in to the Mineral City, stopping for a drink or two at the bar, and then heading for the music hall, buying their tickets from a man posted at the entrance. Glorieta was going to have a full house watching her yet again.

The performance started on time and went well. As always, Glorieta varied her selection of songs a little, and also as always, Longarm enjoyed the show as he watched from backstage. He had been distracted for the past couple of days by Estelle, but he hadn't forgotten how beautiful and talented Glorieta was. He applauded loudly along with the rest of the audience when the curtain came down. By now, Longarm knew to expect an encore. After a few moments, Glorieta stepped through the curtains, waited for the tumult to die down, and sang not one more song but two. The audience loved both of them.

When Glorieta was finished and the show was over, the crowd in the music hall made its way back into the barroom to quench its thirst. McDermott would make a tidy profit tonight. So would Estelle and Branch, Longarm suspected. He waited backstage until Glorieta and Horton were ready to go. It was a short walk to the river, so they hadn't brought a carriage or any other sort of vehicle. The night was a nice one, clear and already cooling off quite a bit from the heat of the day, so the walk would be pleasant.

Glorieta was flushed with excitement and happy that the performance had gone so well. So was Horton. They walked arm-in-arm out the back door of the Mineral City with Longarm right behind them. Movement in the alley that ran behind the saloon caught his eye, and he tensed, his hand going to his gun.

"Take it easy," Salty said as he lounged out of the shadows. "It's just me." He tugged off his battered old hat. "You done mighty good up there, Miss Glorieta."

"Why, thank you, Salty." She leaned forward to give him a peck on his white-bristled cheek. "You're an old dear to say so."

"Just tellin' the truth," the old-timer declared. "All right if I walk back to the boat with you folks?"

"Of course," Horton said. "You don't object, do you, Mr. Parker?"

"Nope." Longarm grinned. "I've gotten a mite fond of this old pelican."

"Old pelican, is it?" Salty blustered. "I'll old pelican you, you young whippersnapper!"

Longarm laughed and said, "Come on, Salty."

The four of them walked toward the riverboat landing. As they approached the dock, Longarm looked over the *Manatee*. Everything seemed to be normal on board the paddle wheeler. Most of its bulk was dark, but lights shone here and there on the boat. There would be people in the salon, and a lookout up in the pilothouse. Some of the crew had been given the night off and allowed to go into Ehrenberg for an evening's entertainment. They would come a-runnin', though, if the boat's whistle blew, because that would mean trouble.

Horton and Glorieta crossed the gangplank to the deck first, followed by Longarm and Salty. They walked the short distance to the companionway that led up to the second deck, where their cabins were located. All four of them started up the steps.

They were halfway up when several figures suddenly appeared at the top of the companionway, silhouetted against the stars and the moonlight behind them. The high-peaked, wide-brimmed shapes of the hats on their heads warned Longarm. He was reaching for his gun when he heard heavy footsteps behind him, at the base of the stairs. A harshly-accented voice said, "Stop right there, gringos." The words were followed immediately by the metallic sound of several guns being cocked.

Salty exclaimed, "What in blue blazes!" and Horton burst out, "Damn it! How dare you—"

"I dare anything I want to, Senor Horton," Don Rafael Aragones said as he stepped into view at the top of the companionway. "And that which I desire, I must possess. That means you, Senorita McCall." Excitement filled Aragones's voice as he went on, "Tonight, the beautiful and famous Arizona Flame will be mine!"

Chapter 10

Longarm didn't move. He stood there, motionless and quiet, while Horton blustered. "Damn you, Aragones!" Horton said. "You can't get away with this! All I have to do is call for help and Captain O'Brien and his crew will be here in seconds!"

"I think not, Senor Horton," Aragones responded calmly. He snapped his fingers, and two of his men stepped forward, shoving a bound figure in front of them. There was enough moonlight for Longarm to be able to make out the angry features of Captain Henry James O'Brien. O'Brien had lost his cap, and a dark blotch on the side of his face could only be blood.

Aragones went on, "Captain O'Brien's men are devoted to him, I think. They will not attack us as long as I hold the captain's life in my hand. Just as your hired gunmen will not reach for their weapons for fear of endangering Senorita McCall."

"Watch who you're callin' a hired gunman, sonny," Salty growled. "I'm a jehu, not a shootist."

"Then if you are also an intelligent man, you will stay out of what does not concern you." Aragones started down the companionway toward Longarm and the others, not hurrying. Arrogance seemed to ooze from his pores. The men who were holding Captain O'Brien captive came after him, followed by two more sombrero-wearing Coltmen who had their guns drawn and ready.

Horton looked past Aragones and said to O'Brien, "Henry, are you all right?"

"It's just a scratch where one of these men struck me with a gun," O'Brien said. "Don't worry about me, Jerome. I'm more concerned about the members of the crew they also attacked."

"No one has been killed," Aragones said sharply. "The captain's men we encountered as we came aboard were simply knocked unconscious and tied up, so that they could not interfere. I am not by nature a violent man."

Salty snorted in contempt at that self-serving statement.

Aragones ignored the old-timer and went on, "My passions run more toward things of beauty, like the lovely Senorita McCall."

"You were the one who tried to have me kidnapped before," Glorieta accused, her voice shaking slightly from the depth of her anger and fear. Mostly anger, though, Longarm thought. Glorieta had the temper to go along with her fiery red hair. "You can't honestly think that I'd ever have anything to do with you, after the things you've done!"

"Senorita, you misunderstand me," Aragones said, lifting a hand to reach out to her. "I want only the best for you. As soon as I saw you in Casa Grande, I knew that I loved you. You will see, when we return to my father's rancho, that I wish only to shower you with my affection and win your heart, so that you will feel the same way about me."

"The only thing I'll ever feel for you is contempt," Glorieta said coldly.

Longarm saw Aragones's face tighten. He might adore Glorieta every bit as much as he claimed to, but her continued rejection of him was making him mad. "It will be different when we are below the border," he said. "You will see."

"I'll kill myself before I ever let you touch me," Glorieta promised.

Longarm wasn't sure it was a good idea for Glorieta to keep prodding Aragones that way. Four gunmen were in front of them, counting the ones who had hold of O'Brien, with three more covering them from behind. Odds like that were well nigh unbeatable in a straight shoot-out. If Aragones took it in his head to kill all five of his prisoners and then make a run for it, there wouldn't be much Longarm could do to stop him.

Except to make sure that Aragones paid for the murders. Longarm was reasonably confident that even if he had a slug or two inside him, he could get his gun out and put a bullet through Aragones's brain before he died.

Maybe it wouldn't come to that. He said, "Look, Aragones, you've got me all wrong. Horton hired me and I'll take my chances straight up, but he ain't payin' me enough to have to go against this many guns. As far as I'm concerned, you can take the girl with my blessing."

"Damn it!" Horton exploded angrily, and Glorieta turned a shocked face toward Longarm. Horton went on, "I had you figured for more of a man than that, Parker. You never showed yellow before."

"Bein' sensible ain't the same thing as bein' yellow," Longarm said.

"In my book it is," Salty said. "I had you figured wrong, too, Parker."

Longarm lifted both hands to shoulder height and started backing away from the others and moving to one side, out of the line of fire. "You do what you want. I'm stayin' out of it."

Horton seethed and cursed. Salty just looked disgusted. Glorieta was afraid and becoming more so by the second as Aragones came closer to her and laughed softly. "Your gallant protector has deserted you, senorita," he said. "Surely you understand now that I am the only man who really cares for you, the only one who will treat you as you truly deserve to be treated."

"Get away from me!" Glorieta said. "Don't touch me!" She suddenly clapped her hands to her face and gave a hysterical scream.

Longarm didn't know if she was faking it or not, but she couldn't have done any better. As all eyes swung toward her, he took one more long step to the side, toward one of Aragones's vaqueros. His left hand closed around the wrist of the man's gun hand and shoved the barrel of the Colt toward the ground. At the same time, Longarm's right hand palmed his revolver from its holster, flipped it around, and smashed the butt of the gun into the man's head, just above the ear so that the sombrero wouldn't blunt the force of the blow. The vaquero went down like a poleaxed steer, leaving Longarm with a clear path to Aragones. He twirled the Colt on his finger and lined the barrel on the young grandee's head.

"Hold it, Aragones!" Longarm barked. "Tell your men to drop their guns, or I'll put a slug right through that thick skull of yours!"

Everyone froze except for O'Brien, who jerked free from the grips of the startled men who were holding him. He turned and smashed a fist into the face of one of the vaqueros. The man sagged to the deck of the boat, stunned. O'Brien stepped over beside Horton, Glorieta, and Salty.

Aragones stood there stiffly, his eyes fixed on the gun that was held rock steady in Longarm's hand. He licked his lips. "You are not a cold-blooded killer, Senor Parker," he said. "You would not murder me."

"You don't know me all that well, old son," Longarm

132

said. "Care to bet your life on how well you can guess what I'd do?"

Clearly, Aragones wasn't willing to do that. But he wasn't ready to give up, either. Probably, no one had ever told him that he couldn't have something he wanted—until now.

"I still have five guns to your one," Aragones pointed out. "If you shoot me, you cannot hope to survive."

"You'll never know whether I survive or not, because you'll be one dead hombre by then."

A laugh came abruptly from Salty. "I knowed you wasn't yellow, Custis. I should've knowed you were just playin' a trick on this fella." He rested his calloused hand on the butt of the old hogleg on his hip. "You just go ahead and start the ball if you want. I'll join right in. I'll bet we can ventilate pert near ever' one o' these fellas 'fore they kill us."

Aragones was looking more and more worried. "But . . . but you said you were not a shootist!" he protested to the old man.

Salty cackled again. "Yeah, but just 'cause I don't make my livin' at it, that don't mean I don't know *how* to shoot!"

The tension stretched out again for a moment following Salty's pronouncement. Then Longarm said again, "Tell your men to drop their guns, Don Rafael. That way, nobody gets killed. Then you take your boys and head for the border."

"Wait just a minute," Horton said. "Kidnapping is a crime, and so is attacking the captain of this boat. These men should go to jail."

O'Brien said, "As long as they go and don't come back, Jerome, it's all right with me. And I'm the one with blood on my head."

Horton looked torn. He didn't want Aragones getting off scot-free after all the trouble he had caused, but at the same time, if Don Rafael would really go back to Mexico, that would be a considerable weight off the shoulders of everyone concerned, including him and Glorieta. After a moment, Horton looked at Glorieta and said, "I suppose it should be up to you, my dear. After all, you're the one who was threatened."

"I never threatened her!" Aragones exclaimed. "Never would I harm one glorious hair on her head!"

Glorieta wouldn't look at him. "Just . . . just make him go away," she said. "I never want to see him again."

Aragones clasped a fist to his breast, as if mortally wounded. Longarm said, "You heard the lady, Don Rafael. Have your men put down their guns, and then all of you get the hell off this boat and out of Arizona Territory." His finger was tight on the trigger of the Colt. "Last chance before all Hades breaks loose."

"All right!" Aragones made a sharp gesture to his men. "Do as the gringo says. We will leave."

Longarm didn't trust him. "Do we have your word of honor on that?"

Aragones hesitated, then grated out, "My word of honor."

"If you break it, I'll see to it that Don Hernando finds out," Longarm said. "I don't reckon he'd take it kindly if he found out you were goin' around lying to folks. He might not care about the kidnapping, but I figure he'd be a mite upset about the other."

From the look on Aragones's face, Longarm thought he was right about the situation. Once the young man had given his word of honor, fear of the old don would make him keep it.

Slowly, carefully, the vaqueros bent and placed their guns on the deck. They helped the men Longarm and O'Brien had knocked down to climb to their feet. All of them backed off, forming a group behind Aragones as he moved slowly toward the gangplank. To Longarm, Don

134

Rafael said, "I hope we meet again someday, Senor Parker. I sincerely hope so."

Without lowering his gun, Longarm said, "Like the old hymn says, Don Rafael, I reckon farther along we'll know more about it."

He kept an eye on the men as they started down the gangplank toward the dock. Horton put an arm around Glorieta's shoulders and hustled her up the stairs, saying, "Come on, my dear, let's get you back to your cabin where you can forget about this dreadful experience."

Longarm wasn't sure how dreadful it had been. It could have turned out a lot worse, he thought. A whole hell of a lot worse . . .

That was when someone yelled from the shadows on the dock, "Look out! He's going for a hideout gun!"

Colt flame gashed the darkness as a gun blasted. Longarm saw Don Rafael Aragones knocked backward by a bullet. Aragones almost fell in the water, but one of his men grabbed him. The others shouted curses in Spanish. Hands darted under *charro* jackets seeking hidden guns. Longarm had suspected that the vaqueros probably were packing more than one iron apiece, but he had hoped that with the explosive situation defused, that wouldn't matter. Now, it suddenly did, as some of the men wheeled back toward the riverboat while the others smashed gunfire toward the dock where the first shot had come from.

Longarm bit back a curse of his own. In a matter of a split second, things had gone to hell, and there was no putting them right again. Now all he could do was try to save his own life and those of Salty and Captain O'Brien. Luckily, Horton and Glorieta were at the top of the companionway and out of the line of fire. He was sure, too, that hearing the burst of gunfire, Horton would rush Glorieta into the safety of her cabin.

In the meantime, bullets were starting to sing a deadly song around Longarm's head. He triggered twice and saw one of the vaqueros tumble off the gangplank to land in the river with a huge splash. Beside him, Salty's old revolver roared and sent another of the gunmen doubling over and off the gangplank. At the same time, Captain O'Brien dropped to one knee and scooped up one of the guns Aragones's men had placed on the deck a couple of minutes earlier. He fired from that position, coolly and accurately squeezing off a pair of shots.

More muzzle flashes bloomed from the dock. The vaquero holding up Aragones grunted and stumbled forward, losing his grip on the young don. Both of them fell, sprawling at the foot of the gangplank. Another man spun off the walkway to plummet into the water as lead fanged into him.

That left just two men still on their feet on the gangplank. With guns snarling, they charged toward the boat, but they never had a chance. Longarm, Salty, and O'Brien fired in unison. The deadly volley knocked both men into the river. The racket died away, leaving only echoes that rolled back from the bluffs behind Ehrenberg.

Longarm's jaw was tight with anger as he stalked down the gangplank. When he reached the spot where Aragones and one of the vaqueros lay, Longarm knelt to check their bodies. Both men were dead. The front of Aragones's white shirt was black with blood in the moonlight. As Longarm rolled the young don onto his back, he saw the revolver still clutched in Aragones's hand. The warning from the dock had been correct. Aragones's wounded pride had proven to be stronger than either his sense of honor or his fear of his father's disapproval. He had decided to try a double cross while he was going down the gangplank.

The figure that came out of the shadows along the dock was holding a gun. "Is he dead?"

Longarm looked up. "That's right."

Tyler Branch knelt on the other side of Aragones's

136

body. "This is the fella you told me about, the one who was trying to grab Miss McCall?"

"That's him," Longarm said with a nod. "Reckon it's a good thing you came along when you did. I figured you'd still be playing poker at the Mineral City."

"The game's still going on," Branch replied. "But only one now, because several of the players dropped out and the others combined the game. Estelle's still in, and I don't like to play against her."

"I noticed."

"So I was heading back to the boat when I came along and saw you and Horton and Miss McCall standing on the deck with those gunmen all around you. I hung back and listened to see if I could tell what was going on. I didn't want to raise a ruckus for fear that they'd start shooting."

"Likely would have," Longarm agreed.

"Then when it looked like they were going to leave, I stayed back in the shadows so I wouldn't spook them. Figured if you were willing to let them go, it wasn't my place to interfere." Branch shrugged. "But then I saw this one pull a gun, and I knew he wasn't going to give up so easily. I wouldn't, if I was after Miss McCall."

Longarm ignored that comment. He straightened and said, "Much obliged for the help. If you hadn't taken a hand, reckon they would've gunned down me and Salty and the captain, then stormed back on board and grabbed the girl. Aragones just couldn't give up, couldn't admit that he'd been beaten."

"A common failing among men who like to gamble," Branch said with a cocky grin.

From the riverboat's second deck, Horton called down, "Is it over?"

Longarm heard a commotion and saw men coming down the street toward the docks, some of them carrying lanterns. The small-scale war that had broken out at the riverboat landing was bound to have attracted a lot of attention, including some from the local law.

"Almost," Longarm said in reply to Horton's question. "But not for a while yet."

The local sheriff's name was Drennan. He was a tall, gaunt old man with white hair and drooping mustaches, as well as eyes that had seen it all in his time. He brought several deputies with him to the riverboat landing and put them to work fishing the bodies of Don Rafael's vaqueros out of the river, then sent one of the bystanders to fetch the undertaker. "He's gonna have plenty of work tonight," Drennan commented dryly. He looked at Horton, who had come back down to the lower deck after Captain O'Brien posted two burly crewmen right outside Glorieta's door with orders to stay there and not let anyone in. "Now, then, Mr. Horton," the local lawman went on, "what's all this about?"

For the next half hour, Horton explained everything that had been going on since Glorieta's singing tour had begun in Casa Grande. Drennan listened intently, nodding his understanding, and when Horton was finished, the old star packer asked, "Then this dust-up tonight don't have anything to do with them bullion robberies that've hit your company?"

Horton shook his head. "Not a thing. This was simply a case of an arrogant, lovestruck young man who couldn't take no for an answer."

"Yeah, there's a bunch o' that in the world, all right." Drennan glanced over at Longarm. "You got the look of a wolf about you, fella. You're the bodyguard Mr. Horton hired for the gal?"

"That's right," Longarm confirmed. If they had been alone, he might have told Drennan who he really was, but in this crowd, it might not be a good idea.

Drennan grunted. "I reckon you're out of a job, then."

Longarm frowned. With everything that had been going on, he'd been too busy to think about that. Aragones represented the only threat to Glorieta. With the young grandee dead, she would be safe now . . . and Horton would no longer require his services.

He had strung out this masquerade as long as he could, Longarm decided. The first chance he got, he was going to discreetly inform Horton that he was really a deputy U.S. marshal investigating the bullion robberies.

Drennan looked around. "Where's the young fella who started the ball?"

Branch stepped forward and said, "That would be me, Sheriff. I saw Aragones going for a hideout gun and called out to warn Mr. Horton and the others."

"From the sound of it, you did more than that, young fella. You accounted for a couple o' them gun throwers yourself."

Branch shrugged. "It seemed like the thing to do at the time."

Drennan regarded him for a moment through shrewd, narrowed eyes. "You know, most o' the time I don't care overmuch for tinhorns. You seem like a decent sort o' hombre, though. Reckon these folks are in your debt."

"*De nada*," Branch said with another shrug.

Drennan turned back to Horton. "Well, everything seems pretty cut-an'-dried. There'll have to be an inquest, but I don't figure there'll be any trouble gettin' a verdict o' justifiable homicide."

"Will we have to stay here?" Horton asked, a frown of concern on his face. "Miss McCall has performances scheduled elsewhere, and I have other business to attend to as well."

Longarm wondered if Horton was referring to the bullion-hauling business. He would find out soon enough, he thought, when he had told Horton who he was and what he was really doing here.

Drennan scratched his bristly chin. "I reckon there ain't no need to hold you up. All of you write up what you told me, sign your statements, and send 'em over to the office. That way this here boat can leave in the mornin' on schedule."

"Thank you, Sheriff," Horton said.

"No need. I know you an' Cap'n O'Brien are straight shooters. I'll handle the coroner."

Drennan and his deputies departed, and the fully-loaded undertaker's wagon trundled away down the street. Horton and O'Brien went about their business, leaving Longarm, Salty, and Branch standing on the deck.

Salty leaned on the railing and said, "Reckon Drennan'll send word to Don Hernando about what happened. That old man ain't gonna be happy when he finds out his boy's dead."

"Aragones gave me no choice," Branch insisted.

"Maybe not, but his pa's liable to regard the whole thing as a blood debt. You best watch your back in the future, young fella. Either that or get the hell out of the Southwest. Don Hernando might send gunmen as far north as Montana to get you . . . but he might not go to that much trouble."

"I don't believe in running," Branch said coldly, "and as for watching my back . . . I'm already in the habit of doing that."

Salty looked the other direction at Longarm. "You're liable to come in for some o' this, too. Don Hernando might blame you for his boy gettin' ventilated, as well as Branch."

"I reckon he'll do whatever he thinks he's got to do," Longarm said. "And we'll burn that bridge when we come to it."

Chapter 11

Late that night, well after midnight, Longarm left his cabin and went along the deck to the door of Jerome Horton's cabin. He lifted his hand and was about to knock softly when sounds from the dock caught his attention. He turned and looked over the railing to see several men carrying large crates from wagons parked at the landing. The men brought the crates, which obviously were quite heavy, to the broader gangplank by which cargo was loaded and unloaded. The big wooden boxes were brought on board.

Longarm had intended to have a frank discussion with Horton about the situation, but that could wait, he decided. He was curious and wanted to find out what was going on. One answer had suggested itself to him already, and he wanted to see if he was right.

Moving with cat-footed grace that was unusual in such a big man, Longarm went to the companionway and started down the steps, hugging the wall so that he could stay in the shadows. When he got to the bottom, he took off his Stetson and edged an eye around a corner so that he could peer along the deck toward the cargo area at the boat's stern. He saw a tall, erect figure wearing a beaver hat standing there, watching the crates being loaded. That was Jerome Horton, Longarm realized. And next to Horton was the stockier, solid shape of Captain O'Brien.

With a grim smile tugging at his mouth, Longarm moved up behind the two men. "Loadin' bullion in the dead o' night," he said quietly. "Not a bad idea, but there's still bound to be quite a few folks who know about it."

Both Horton and O'Brien started as Longarm spoke. As the captain turned toward him, Longarm saw that O'Brien had a gun in his hand. "Blast it!" he exclaimed. "Sneaking up on a man is a good way to get yourself shot, Mr. Parker."

"I reckon you're right," Longarm muttered. "Sorry. But you fellas seem to be doing some sneaking of your own."

"You know how much trouble I've had with bullion shipments recently," Horton said. "It seemed that loading this shipment as discreetly as possible was a good idea. Not that it's any of your business, Parker." Horton's voice became sharper as he added the last statement.

"Actually, it is my business," Longarm said. "And the name ain't Parker. It's Long. Deputy United States Marshal Custis Long."

Even in the shadows, Longarm could tell that Horton and O'Brien were staring at him in surprise. "Deputy Marshal?" Horton repeated. "But how . . . ?"

"Why should we take your word for that?" O'Brien asked.

"You don't have to." Before leaving his cabin, Longarm had taken the leather folder from the hidden pocket in his saddlebags. Now he handed it to Horton. "There's my badge and bona fides. I've been on this case ever since I ran into you in Casa Grande, Horton. Signin' on to look after Miss McCall was just something I decided to use as a cover when the opportunity came up."

It was so late the moon had set, but there was enough

starlight still in the sky so that it struck reflections off the badge pinned inside the leather folder when Horton opened it. He couldn't read the documents, but the badge seemed to be enough to convince him that Longarm was telling the truth. "My God," he murmured. "I never dreamed you were anything but a gunman, even when you went with the posse after those thieves."

"Would've been nice if we could have rounded them up then. Too bad it didn't work out that way."

"Then you didn't really care about Aragones—?"

"I wouldn't say that." Longarm's voice was hard, flinty. "I don't hold with tryin' to kidnap women, no matter what the reason. And once Don Rafael's boys had tried a couple of times to kill me, I had a sort of natural dislike for the hombre. I'm glad I was able to help protect her from him, even though that wasn't my real job."

"But now, with Aragones's threat disposed of, you decided it was time to reveal your true identity?" O'Brien asked.

Longarm took the folder back from Horton and slipped it in his pocket. "Yep. I was on my way to Horton's cabin to hash it all out when I heard this cargo coming on board. When I saw the two of you, I figured it had to be more bullion."

Horton took off his hat and wearily rubbed a hand over his face. "It's a good-sized shipment," he said as he replaced the hat. "I can't afford to lose it, or the others we'll be taking on as we proceed upriver."

Longarm frowned. "You're pickin' up the bullion as you go *up*river, not down?"

"That's right. There will be shipments coming on board at La Paz and Hardyville, too. We'll have a large amount of gold and silver on board when the *Manatee* turns around at Hardyville."

O'Brien added, "And then we'll run like blazes back to Yuma. We can make better time going downstream rather than up, so Jerome and I decided to pick up the bullion on the way."

Deep in thought, Longarm tugged on his earlobe for a moment and then rasped a thumbnail along the line of his jaw. "If you don't stop except for wood, you can make the downriver run pretty fast, all right. But not fast enough to outrun that gang of thieves."

"We'll stick close to the middle of the river," Horton insisted. "The only way they can stop us is by coming after us in boats. And I'll match Captain O'Brien's skill against anyone's when it comes to running the river."

Longarm nodded slowly. The plan was risky, but they might be able to pull it off. There was no way to carry the bullion, no matter when it was loaded, without taking some chances. But even if these shipments got through safely, that wouldn't help Longarm do his job, which was to bring the gang to justice. As long as the owlhoots were on the loose, Horton's operation would be in danger.

"I plan to have a caravan of heavily guarded wagons waiting for us in Yuma when we get back," Horton went on. "They'll carry the bullion to Tucson, where it will be loaded on the train and shipped to the mint in Denver."

"What about next time?" Longarm asked, giving voice to the thoughts that were running through his head. "You might dodge the gang once or twice, but they're not going to give up and go away."

"You can't be sure of that. They've made a good haul from me already." Horton's voice was bitter. "Maybe that will be enough to satisfy them."

"The marshal's probably right, Jerome," O'Brien put in. "Men like those robbers are usually too greedy to give up easily."

Horton spread his hands. "But what can we do other than try to avoid them?"

"I've been thinkin' about that," Longarm said, "and I reckon I might have an idea . . ."

The *Manatee* pulled away from the Ehrenberg landing early the next morning, as scheduled. The crates containing the bullion had been covered with canvas and were not too noticeable. As Longarm stood at the railing and watched the town receding behind the boat, he wondered if outlaw eyes were studying the riverboat through field glasses at that very moment. If the bullion thieves were keeping a watch on the boat and waiting for the right moment to strike, as seemed likely, they would notice that more cargo had been loaded on board. Longarm didn't doubt that for a moment.

All along, he had suspected that the gang was getting information from someone who knew what Horton was doing. Otherwise, they would not have known when the bullion shipments were being moved. Horton and O'Brien had kept their plans as secret as possible, but secrets could always leak out. No scheme was foolproof. A deckhand, somebody who worked at the riverboat landing, an employee at one of the mines . . . anybody could have passed the word along and let the gang know that the *Manatee* would be carrying a fortune in bullion on its trip back downriver.

Longarm was counting on that, in fact.

Soft footsteps sounded beside him. He looked over and raised an eyebrow in surprise as Glorieta McCall leaned on the railing. "Mornin'," Longarm said. "You're up mighty early today."

"I didn't feel like sleeping," she said with a smile. "I'm just so relieved that all the trouble is over."

Longarm didn't think it was over, not by a long shot, but he knew what she meant and didn't disagree with her. As far as Glorieta was concerned, Don Rafael Aragones had represented the only real threat.

"I'm glad you're still here," she went on. "I was afraid

that you would have left, now that I don't need you to guard me anymore."

"My horse is still in Yuma," Longarm pointed out. "I don't have much choice but to finish the trip."

Glorieta laughed. "And here I was, thinking that perhaps it was my company you couldn't get enough of. I should have known better, though." She lowered her voice. "Ever since you met that Estelle Henry, you've neglected me terribly, Custis."

He looked out at the water as the river slid by. "Well, I'm sorry about that. Estelle and me, we're old friends, you know. Lot of old times to catch up on."

Glorieta gave a brittle-sounding laugh. "I'll bet."

"It's the truth."

"Even so, I miss you, Custis." She sighed. "I suppose I'll just have to pay more attention to that handsome young Tyler Branch. He seems quite taken with me. Not the way Don Rafael was, of course. Mr. Branch is a gentleman. He would never kidnap a lady or try to force himself on her."

"No, I reckon not," Longarm said. "But you'd better be careful. You and me took some chances we shouldn't have. Horton's got other things on his mind, but that don't mean he's forgotten about you. He might not like it if you took up with Branch."

"Jerome's not my father, no matter what he thinks," Glorieta said sharply. "And I'll take up, as you put it, with anybody I want to."

Longarm shrugged. "That's your decision. I'm just sayin' you might want to think about it, that's all."

"I'll think about it . . . and then I'll do what I want." With that, she turned and walked away, her skirts swirling around her ankles.

Longarm watched her go and gave a little shake of his head. Maybe it wasn't intentional, but Glorieta had a way of stirring things up around her. First Aragones's obsession with her had complicated Longarm's job and put his life in danger more than once, and now Glorieta was threatening to cause trouble between Jerome Horton and Tyler Branch. It would sure simplify matters, Longarm thought, if the whole business between men and women wasn't so likely to make hell go to popping.

But on the other hand, he wasn't sure he would want to live in a world where that was true . . .

For the next week, as the *Manatee* steamed upriver, Longarm spent time with Salty, swapping stories with the old-timer, talked to Captain O'Brien about all the exotic places the mariner had visited and all the strange things he'd seen, and kept an eye on the bullion, just in case somebody on board the riverboat decided to help themselves to a bar or two. He also played cards with Tyler Branch, who seemed surprised that Longarm had the skill to hold his own in the game, and he made love with Estelle Henry, who couldn't seem to get enough of both reminiscing and romping.

He saw hardly anything of Glorieta McCall, who spent most of her time in her cabin. When she did come out, she flirted with Branch, who seemed to enjoy her attention and returned the flirting.

Jerome Horton worried. When he wasn't fretting about the bullion, he was concerned about the growing relationship between Glorieta and Branch. Longarm couldn't help him with that part of it, but he assured Horton that the bullion was safe—for the moment—and that his fledgling plan to trap the thieves was coming together.

La Paz, like Ehrenberg, had been founded because of the mines in the area. It had no music hall or theater, but it did have a good-sized saloon. That was where Glorieta performed. Despite the growing tension between her and Horton, she sang her heart out on stage, as usual. Longarm watched from the audience this time, instead of staying backstage where he could get to her quickly in case of trouble, and he enjoyed the show as much as ever. He was sure that by the time she got back to Tucson, she would have no trouble performing there, no matter how large the crowds were. Her confidence had grown by leaps and bounds during this trip across southern Arizona Territory and up the Colorado River. In that respect, the trip had been a success.

The jury was still out on the bullion business. More crates were brought on board at La Paz and added to the pile underneath the canvas, again in the middle of the night. Whether they would ever reach Yuma was still open to doubt.

Longarm watched the river as the *Manatee* headed north, and Captain O'Brien's prediction that the water level would fall turned out to be right. The Colorado sunk lower between the bluffs that bordered it. The blue water turned a roiled brown in places, indicating that there were sandbars not far below the surface. O'Brien and his pilots steered skillfully around them, and though the riverboat could not proceed at quite as fast a pace, there was always a channel deep enough for it to get through.

"My bones tell me there'll be rain in the mountains before much longer," O'Brien commented to Longarm as the two of them stood one day on the texas deck, just below the level of the pilothouse. "When that happens, the river will rise again."

"We don't want that to happen too soon," Longarm said. "I don't want all the sandbars covered up."

O'Brien looked over at him through narrowed eyes. "What? Why not?"

"Remember what I said about havin' an idea of how to deal with that gang of bullion thieves?" When O'Brien nodded, Longarm went on, "I reckon they're going to hit us on our way back downriver. There'll be too much gold and silver on the boat for them to resist the temptation.

148

But I want to pick the time when they come after us, not the other way around."

"How are you going to manage that?" O'Brien asked curiously.

"When they see the *Manatee* hung up on a sandbar, they'll figure we're sitting ducks out here."

O'Brien stared at him. "I've never run aground on a sandbar in my life!" he said, sounding offended by the very idea.

"But you could if you wanted to."

After a moment, understanding began to dawn in O'Brien's eyes. "You want me to find a sandbar, steer the *Manatee* as close to it as possible without actually grounding it, and bring the boat to a shuddering halt. Anyone watching us would think we were stuck!"

Longarm nodded. "That's the idea. And when the gang comes after us, we'll be waiting for them."

"It could work," O'Brien said. "Damned if it couldn't! Have you told Jerome about this idea?"

"Not yet, but I'm going to. Until the last minute, when we have to let Joe Cleghorn and the rest of your crew in on it, nobody's going to know about it except the three of us, and maybe Salty. That old pelican's mighty handy to have around when trouble starts to pop."

"One more thing: Do you think the gang already has someone on board?"

"I wouldn't be surprised," Longarm said, his face grim. "You've got a couple of dozen regular passengers, and any one of 'em could be working with the thieves. So when Hades breaks loose, we'll have to be on the lookout for trouble from the inside as well as out."

"Joe and the rest of my lads will acquit themselves well in a fight, you can be sure of that," O'Brien declared. "They've cleaned up trouble from the Singapore Passage to the Cape of Good Hope."

"Good," Longarm said with a curt nod. "I'll be countin' on them."

The *Manatee* chugged on toward Hardyville, where the Colorado River finally grew too narrow and shallow for paddle wheelers. Back in the days before the Late Unpleasantness, an army major and a party of volunteer scouts had taken small boats down the Colorado all the way from above the great canyon down to the Gulf of California, riding the rapids and risking all the dangers the river held. They had helped establish the fact that the Colorado was navigable by steamboat this far upriver, which had led to the regular runs by the *Manatee* and the other paddle wheelers that traveled between Yuma and Hardyville, Arizona Territory, and those who had settled it, owed a debt to those daring explorers.

The bluffs closed in at Hardyville, leaving room for the steamboat to turn around and head back downriver. Before it did so, however, Glorieta McCall had one last performance scheduled. Again, it was in a saloon, the Golden Argosy, owned by an Irishman named Jack Byrne. Longarm and Salty tagged along with Horton and Glorieta when they went to the place. Byrne didn't stock any Maryland rye in the Golden Argosy, but his whiskey was passable, Longarm found. He and the old-timer stood at the bar to watch Glorieta's performance that night. Longarm felt a little twinge of regret as the last notes of Glorieta's final song faded away. There was a good chance he might not ever hear her sing again.

Glorieta was more her old self as they returned to the boat that night. She hung on Horton's arm and laughed excitedly as she talked about how well the performance had gone. Horton beamed with pride, just like he really was her father. Longarm and Salty came along behind. The old man said fondly, "It's good to see that gal so happy. There's just somethin' about her that makes me want to see her get what she wants out o' life."

"I know what you mean," Longarm agreed. "Horton seems to feel the same way about her."

"Yeah. Now if he can just get that bullion back downriver without them owlhoots comin' after it . . ."

Longarm looked over at him. "You know about the bullion, Salty?"

The old-timer snorted. "O' course I know about it. I ain't blind. We been talkin' on cargo every time we stop. Makes sense that it's gold an' silver, since totin' the stuff is Horton's business."

Longarm hung back a little, letting Horton and Glorieta get farther ahead so that he could still see them but far enough so they were out of earshot. In a quiet voice, he said, "That bullion is my business, too."

Salty looked sharply at him. "You're a lawman?"

"What makes you say that?"

"If you're really interested in that bullion, you got to be either a star packer or one o' the gang, and I know that ain't true. I was sort of wonderin' if maybe you carried a badge, Custis, when you stuck around after that dust-up with Don Rafael was over."

"Name's Custis Long. Deputy U.S. marshal out of Denver."

"Uh-huh. Can't say as I'm surprised. You never really struck me as the gunman sort, even though you're mighty handy with that Colt o' yours. You were just pretendin' to stand guard over the girl, when you were really watchin' over the bullion."

"Not completely," Longarm said. "I didn't want Aragones getting his hands on Glorieta."

"Me, neither. Well, what do you do now, Mr. Lawman? Guard the gold an' silver and hope them desperadoes don't come after it?"

"Actually, the captain and I have been talking about setting a trap for them."

"O'Brien's in on this, is he? How about Horton?"

151

"He knows who I am now," Longarm admitted. "He didn't at first, though."

"What's the matter? Didn't you trust him? Think maybe he had somethin' to do with his own mule trains and wagons gettin' raided?"

"Things like that have happened before," Longarm pointed out. "But no, I didn't really mistrust Horton. I just wanted to work undercover for a while. It's worked before. It didn't this time, but hell, I didn't lose anything by it, either."

"No, I reckon not. How come you've spilled the truth to me?"

"Because when the showdown comes, I want another good man to back my play."

Salty looked up at him. "I'm much obliged that you feel that way about me, Custis. I'll try not to let you down." He leaned closer. "Now, what's the plan?"

"We're going to give those bullion thieves a nice fat target," Longarm said. "Too fat for them to resist . . ."

As the *Manatee* steamed south from Hardyville the next morning, Longarm stood near the stern and looked past the canvas-covered pile of crates toward the mountains in the distance. Dark clouds loomed over the peaks. As Captain O'Brien had predicted, rain was moving in. If there were storms in the mountains, in a day or two the level of the river would rise. From time to time, enough rain fell to make the Colorado flood. Longarm didn't expect that to happen this time, but he was a little nervous about the possibility. A flood would make the sandbars disappear far underneath the surface and ruin his plan to lure the bullion gang into a trap.

After Longarm had explained things to O'Brien, during the rest of the trip upriver the captain had been on the lookout for a suitable place to set the trap. Longarm knew the place O'Brien had selected. The riverboat would reach it about two days out of Hardyville.

Those two days dragged by for Longarm. He tried not to let anyone see how tense he was getting, but Estelle noticed. Even though their lovemaking sessions were as passionate and athletic as always, she could tell that he was distracted. The second night after leaving Hardyville, when they had been romping for a while in her dimly lit cabin, she rested her forearms on Longarm's chest and looked down into his eyes. His shaft was still buried inside her, though it was beginning to soften after yet another climax. She said, "What's wrong, Custis? You're about as jumpy these days as a long-tailed cat on a porch full of rocking chairs."

Longarm chuckled. "It always was hard to hide anything from you, Stella Jean."

He felt her stiffen. "It's Estelle now. You know that, Custis."

"Sorry. I reckon I just got carried away with rememberin' those old times."

"And I didn't mean to snap at you." Her tone was softer now. "But despite all the fine times I had with you, my life wasn't very good back then. In fact, it was bad enough I promised myself I'd never be poor and helpless again. That's why I've worked so hard to get where I am. I won't ever ever go back to the sort of life I lived in West Virginia."

"I'd never ask you to," Longarm said. "I don't reckon I'd go back, either, even if I could."

She leaned down to kiss him, and her hips began to work back and forth. The wet heat that created around his organ made it start to swell again.

"Let's forget about the past," she said breathlessly as he began thrusting in and out of her. "And the future. All I care about is the here and now . . ."

* * *

Lightning flickered in the clouds that hovered over the mountains to the north. Longarm glanced at it as he paced the deck of the riverboat. So far, the river hadn't risen any. He checked the landmarks the paddle wheeler was passing. The place where O'Brien would pretend to run the boat aground was coming up in another mile or two. Longarm looked at the bluffs to the right and left of the river. Were the bullion thieves out there somewhere, watching? He sure as hell hoped so, or he was going to feel like a mighty big fool.

The burly, craggy-faced Joe Cleghorn came along the deck toward him. "Cap'n O'Brien says to tell you that everything is ready," Cleghorn said.

Longarm gave a curt nod. "You know the plan?"

It was Cleghorn's turn to nod. "Yeah, the cap'n explained everything to me a little while ago. I passed the word to a few trusted men, and they'll take command of the rest of the crew if those damned pirates hit us. We'll give 'em a warm reception, you can count on that."

"Sounds good," Longarm said with a nod. He left Cleghorn on the lower deck and walked up to Horton's cabin.

Horton answered Longarm's quiet knock. "Are we nearly there?" he asked.

"That's right," Longarm said. "Glorieta's in her cabin?"

"Yes, and I've told her to stay there, no matter what happens. She's quite curious, and she was a little upset with me when I wouldn't tell her what's going on. I just hope she'll understand when I explain it all later."

"I reckon she will," Longarm said. He didn't know if Glorieta would understand or not, and right now he didn't care. That was Horton's concern.

Longarm went to the bow and rested his hands on the railing. The riverboat swept around a bend and entered a long straightaway. Up ahead, several patches of brown water marked the locations of sandbars. A blue channel

154

wound between them. Up in the pilothouse, O'Brien would be taking the helm himself, if all was going according to plan. At the stern, the giant paddle wheel threw water high in the air as it churned along. Longarm's hands tightened on the railing as the *Manatee* passed several of the sandbars. The boat was drifting gradually to the right, as if the man at the wheel wasn't paying close attention to what he was doing. It moved closer to one of the stretches of brown water.

Longarm saw the sandbar passing just to starboard. Suddenly, the riverboat lurched as the engines were thrown into reverse and then killed. Longarm steadied himself against the rail, knowing that O'Brien had barked the appropriate orders through the speaking tube that connected the pilothouse with the engine room. To anyone watching from the bluffs, it would appear that the *Manatee* had run aground on the sandbar and gotten stuck. Longarm started to turn away from the rail.

Something round and hard pressed against the back of his neck. Longarm stiffened, recognizing the feel of a gun barrel.

"Don't move, Custis," Tyler Branch said. "I like you, and I'd hate like hell to have to blow your brains out."

Chapter 12

Longarm felt anger burning through him in a fierce blaze.
Branch! Tyler Branch was one of the bullion gang. That
revelation was a stunning disappointment. Longarm had
liked the young man, despite the fact that Branch was a
professional gambler. And though he had never been able
to figure out why, Branch still reminded him of someone
he knew.

"I don't reckon I want you shooting me, either, old
son," Longarm said, keeping his voice cool and steady.
"Just tell me what you want."

"Head up to the pilothouse," Branch ordered. "You're
going to tell Captain O'Brien to order his crew not to
resist."

"When the rest of the gang comes on board to steal that
bullion?" Longarm guessed.

"You know too much, Custis. You're a lawman, aren't
you?" Branch didn't sound particularly upset by the idea,
or surprised, either.

"Looks like both of us been wearin' false faces."

Branch prodded the back of Longarm's neck with the
gun barrel. "Up the stairs. Now."

As Longarm turned toward the companionway, he saw

men on horseback starting down a trail along the bluff on the eastern side of the river. They would be the rest of the bullion thieves, he thought. Branch must have signaled to them to move in already. He wondered if the young man was the leader of the gang. It was certainly possible.

Longarm was fairly sure of one thing: Branch didn't know about the plan he had set up with O'Brien, Horton, and Salty. Even though Branch had the drop on him, it could still work. Joe Cleghorn and the rest of the crew would be armed and waiting for the bullion raiders when they came aboard. Longarm had to keep Branch from getting to O'Brien, though. If he could just turn the tables somehow . . .

Longarm was halfway up the companionway when he stumbled, catching his foot on a riser and going to one knee. The move was deliberate, of course, but it looked real enough to fool Branch and make him hesitate to fire for the split-second that Longarm needed. Branch started to exclaim, "What—" when Longarm twisted around and knocked the gambler's gun arm aside with a sweep of his elbow. Longarm's left hand darted down, closing over the cylinder of the pistol that Branch held. A gunshot now would warn the raiders, but Branch couldn't fire as long as Longarm's fingers were clamped around the cylinder in an iron grip. Longarm threw a hard right jab at Branch's face.

Branch jerked his head aside so that Longarm's fist just grazed his ear. He brought his knee up, aiming the blow at Longarm's groin. The big lawman turned so that Branch's knee slammed against his hip instead. That was still enough to stagger him. He lost his balance for real this time, falling down the steps. He grabbed Branch, though, and took the gambler with him. Both men tumbled wildly toward the lower deck.

Longarm lost his grip on the pistol, but so did Branch. The gun clattered away. They rolled over as they reached the bottom of the companionway, each man struggling desperately to gain the advantage. Longarm got a hand around Branch's throat, but a second later Branch sunk a fist in Longarm's belly, knocking the wind out of him and loosening his hold. Branch splayed the fingers of his other hand over Longarm's face and clawed at his eyes. Longarm had to twist away.

That gave Branch a chance to roll in the opposite direction. He came up with a knife glittering in his hand, a razor-sharp dirk that he had slipped from a sheath on his forearm, under the sleeve of his coat. He slashed at Longarm's face as the deputy marshal came up on one knee. Longarm threw himself backward to avoid the blade. He landed heavily on his back, but as he did so, he kicked upward. The heel of his boot caught Branch on the wrist. The knife spun out of his hand.

Branch kicked at Longarm then, a vicious blow that would have taken Longarm's head off his shoulders if it had connected. Longarm flung himself out of the way and surged to his feet, swinging a punch while Branch was still off-balance from the missed kick. The blow connected solidly with Branch's jaw and sent him flying backward toward the railing. For a second Longarm thought Branch was going to hit the rail and go right on over, but the gambler caught himself at the last instant. Longarm rushed him, but Branch darted aside. Longarm hit the railing and bounced off. Branch's fist smacked into the side of his head, just above the ear. Branch tried to close in, but Longarm threw out an elbow that caught him in the solar plexus and made him go pale as he stumbled back a step.

"I'll . . . kill you!" Branch gasped.

"You can try . . . old son," Longarm replied, equally breathless.

Branch's elegant good looks were deceptive. He was really as tough as whang leather and packed plenty of

159

power in his punches. Longarm had a little advantage in height and reach, but Branch was a shade faster with his fists. For a long moment, both men stood toe-to-toe, slugging it out, giving and receiving as good as they got. Blood dripped from a cut on Longarm's forehead into his eyes. He blinked rapidly to clear them as he threw a wild right and left, both of which were guided by sheer instinct and connected with Branch's face. Branch sagged back against the railing, gulping down air and trying to cling to consciousness.

Longarm had lost track of what else might be happening on board the riverboat, and right then, he didn't care. This battle between him and Branch had become personal and swelled to such proportions that he couldn't allow himself to worry about anything else. He wanted to polish off Branch—then he could turn his attention to other matters. He moved toward the rail, his right arm cocked and his big fist poised to deliver the finishing stroke. Branch was too groggy to defend himself.

At the last instant, Longarm saw Branch's eyes flick past him, gazing at something over his shoulder. He knew it wasn't a trick; Branch was too far gone for that. But Longarm's momentum was going forward, and it was too late for him to stop himself.

Something exploded on the back of his head, showering him with a flood of blackness that washed him away to oblivion.

Climbing back into awareness after being knocked out was always a painful process. This time was no different as Longarm's brain slowly came to life. At first he knew only a sick, nauseated feeling, and then light began to seep around the lids of his closed eyes. The glare just made him more ill. Acting out of a reflex that made him want to get away from the brightness, he started to roll onto his side. That sent fresh waves of pain rolling through him.

A voice cut through the pain. "Please don't move, Custis. After all we've meant to each other, I don't want to shoot you. But I will if I have to."

Not Tyler Branch this time. Longarm's sluggish mental processes were working well enough for him to realize that. It was a woman's voice that had spoken. A voice that he had heard lifted many times in beautiful song . . .

He raised his head, blinked his eyes open, and stared up at Glorieta McCall.

The Arizona Flame was as beautiful as ever. She wore a dark green gown and had her fiery red hair loose around her shoulders. She also had a gun in her hand, the barrel pointing at Longarm. He recognized it as his own Colt. Glorieta handled it with ease. Clearly, this wasn't the first time she had pointed a gun at someone.

"Well, I'll be a son of a bitch," Longarm rasped. "Was *everybody* in on this holdup?"

"Just lie there quietly, Custis," Glorieta said. "It'll all be over soon, and then we'll go on our way. No one else has to be hurt."

"Who's been hurt so far?" Longarm asked.

"That man Cleghorn . . . I'm afraid Tyler had to shoot him. I don't know if he's dead or not. And another member of the crew was killed when he tried to fight. The rest of them surrendered when Captain O'Brien told them to."

"Branch got to O'Brien after you clouted me over the head." It was a statement, not a question. "I'm a mite surprised O'Brien gave in. Reckon he values the lives of his crewmen more than he does that bullion."

"He's a reasonable man," Glorieta said. "Money's not worth dying over. Unless, of course, you've never had any of it. Then you'll do whatever it takes to get it."

"What about the passengers?"

"They're all disarmed and being held in the salon, including Jerome."

Longarm felt sorry for Horton, but there was nothing he could do for the man right now except try to turn the tables on the raiders. His eyes cut around. He was lying on his side with his back against the bulkhead on the lower deck. Glorieta stood several feet away, out of reach if he tried to kick her or make a grab for the gun. From where he was, Longarm couldn't see the cargo area at the stern, but he heard voices coming from there. The bullion thieves, loading the crates onto small boats they had rowed out into the river from shore. He could hear the creak of oarlocks and the splash of water as the oars bit into it, and from that he figured out what the thieves were doing.

"What did the gang do, stash boats all up and down the river?"

"Only in certain locations that seemed likely places where the *Manatee* could be boarded. Tyler rode up and down the Colorado a couple of times several weeks ago, just figuring things out."

"He knew that long ago that Horton planned to pick up a fortune in bullion on this trip, because you told him."

Glorieta smiled. "Of course. Those other robberies netted us some good hauls, but this riverboat trip was always intended to be the big payoff. Jerome always talks to me when he's worried, and this trip has been on his mind for a while."

Longarm bit back a curse. He hated being fooled, and Glorieta had deceived him as well as Horton. He might have been more suspicious of the young woman if she hadn't seemed like such a victim, what with Aragones being after her . . .

"Aragones," Longarm said. "He wasn't part of this, was he?"

Glorieta's face hardened. "That meddling greaser!" she

practically spat. "Everything was set up, and then he had to see me in Casa Grande and go and fall in love with me!"

"Then that part of it was real, not a trick or a double cross?"

"Aragones really did try to kidnap me, all three times. He could have ruined everything. I'm glad he was so stubborn about it that he finally got himself killed."

Longarm closed his eyes for a second. He didn't feel any more kindly toward Don Rafael Aragones, but at least the young grandee had been honest about what he wanted. He hadn't set out to fool everyone with whom he came in contact.

"I'm feelin' a mite sick," Longarm said when he opened his eyes again. "You mind if I sit up?"

"Yes, I do mind," Glorieta snapped. "You stay there just like you are. You've caused enough trouble, Custis. Lying to me like that, claiming to be my bodyguard when you were actually a lawman!"

"Branch told you about that, did he?"

"Tyler tells me everything, just like I tell him everything. Except for the things you and I did together. I don't think he would enjoy hearing all those details."

"What do you plan to do when the bullion's all unloaded?" Longarm asked. "Shoot me so that Branch won't ever find out?"

"That's not necessary. Tyler may not like it much, but he knows I'll do whatever I have to in order to get what I want. He and I are just alike in that respect."

"Damn it, girl!" Longarm's hands clenched into fists, and he couldn't stop himself from rising up a bit from his prone position. His anger wouldn't let him stay still. "You could've had everything you wanted without killin' and robbin'! That voice of yours would've made you rich. The Arizona Flame really would've been famous!"

The Colt trembled a little in Glorieta's hand. "Shut up!

163

I don't want to hear about that or even think about it! My mother used to make me sing for her and all the men she brought in. They thought it was so precious that the whore's daughter had such a beautiful voice! If she'd never left my father, it never would have happened. None of the things that happened to me would have—"

She stopped short, reached up to her neck with her free hand, and pulled a locket from under her dress. A sharp tug broke the chain it was on, and she threw the locket to the deck and brought her foot down on it, breaking it. She kicked the busted locket behind her.

"My mother can burn in hell," she said. "She died a penniless, broken-down whore because she couldn't stand the life my father wanted her to live out in the desert, while he looked for gold. She would have been better off staying there with him."

Longarm was looking past her toward the bow of the boat. A few moments earlier, he had caught a flicker of movement there. Now he saw it again and realized that there was a fringe of bushy white whiskers at the corner of the front cabin. Someone was standing there, just out of sight. Longarm could think of only one passenger on the *Manatee* who had a beard like that.

Glorieta had said everyone on the riverboat had been captured by the raiders. Longarm saw now that that wasn't true. Salty must have dodged them somehow, because he was edging around the corner behind Glorieta. Longarm didn't look directly at the old-timer for fear of tipping off Glorieta that someone was behind her, but he watched from the corner of his eye as Salty began creeping along the deck toward them.

To cover any noises the old man might make, Longarm said, "You really think your pa would approve of what you're doin', Glorieta? No matter what your ma did, he wouldn't have wanted you to spend your life robbin' and killin'."

164

"Don't talk to me about my father," Glorieta said. "He never knew anything about it. In his way, he was just as big a fool as my mother was. He thought he was going to strike it rich. I never knew him, but she talked about him until the day she died. She never forgave him for holding so tight to his dreams. And those dreams betrayed him, just like hers forced her into the life she led." She shook her head. "I don't want to talk about this. It's all in the past now. I'm not thinking about anything except the future and how rich I'm going to be. Tyler and I are taking our share of the loot and heading for the border. We'll settle down in Mexico and never come back."

Salty was only a few yards behind her now. Longarm saw him look down at the deck, at the locket Glorieta had broken and cast aside. The old man raised his eyes to her and spread his arms. He took one more step and then lunged forward, tackling Glorieta from behind and reaching around her for the gun.

Glorieta let out a startled scream as Salty grabbed her and forced the gun toward the deck. Her finger jerked the trigger, sending a slug into the deck boards as the gun blasted. Longarm had started to scramble to his feet as soon as Salty made his move, but he was still groggy and his muscles didn't work quite as smoothly and efficiently as usual. That delay gave Glorieta time enough to writhe free of Salty's grip and swing around toward him. The Colt boomed again. Salty grunted and staggered back a step.

Longarm reached out and clamped a hand on Glorieta's shoulder. She gasped as he hauled her around. He didn't give her a chance to bring the gun to bear on him. His fist lashed out and clipped her on the jaw. Her eyes rolled up in her head as she slumped against the bulkhead, stunned.

Longarm ripped the revolver out of her hand as she slid down the wall to the deck. He leaped past her and caught hold of Salty's arm to steady him as he leaned against the bulkhead. Blood showed crimson on the old man's shirt and buckskin vest.

"How bad are you hit?" Longarm asked.

Salty's leathery face was pale under its permanent tan. He shook his head and said, "I'm all right. The slug just gouged a chunk o' meat outta my side. What about the girl?"

Longarm glanced over his shoulder at Glorieta. "She's out cold. Don't reckon she'll be coming around for a few minutes." He heard alarmed shouts coming from the riverboat's stern. "You feel strong enough to keep an eye on her?"

Salty jerked his head in a nod. "Sure. You go on, son. Do what you can to stop Branch and the rest o' them owlhoots."

Longarm squeezed the old man's shoulder with his free hand and then turned to run toward the stern. He had gone only a few yards when he saw a hard-faced man in range clothes coming toward him, brandishing a revolver. The outlaw skidded to a stop and brought up the gun. Longarm dropped to one knee as the owlhoot triggered a shot at him. The wind-rip of the bullet seemed to tug at Longarm's ear. He fired once in return and was rewarded by the sight of the bullion thief doubling over in pain. The man's gun slipped from his fingers as he fell to the deck.

Longarm was up and running again, but instead of going all the way to the stern of the boat, he bounded up a narrow companionway that led to the second deck. If he could get above the outlaws he would have a better chance against them in a shoot-out. As he took the stairs three at a time, he fished out fresh cartridges from the pocket of his jeans and thumbed them through the Colt's loading gate after dumping the empty brass. He normally carried the gun with the hammer resting on an empty cylinder, but now all six chambers were filled.

A man appeared at the top of the companionway and lined his sights on Longarm. Before he could fire, another figure loomed up behind him and smashed something against the back of his head. The man tumbled down the steps toward Longarm, who jumped aside. He saw the way the outlaw's skull was caved in and knew that was one more owlhoot permanently out of the fight.

At the top of the companionway, Joe Cleghorn grinned down at Longarm. There was blood on his face and on his shirt, but he seemed spry enough at the moment. He had a piece of wood from the engine room firebox in his hand that he had used as a makeshift but very effective club.

"Hello, Long," he said. "Me and the boys've been waitin' for something to distract those damned lubbers so we could jump 'em. You'll see a fine fight now!"

From the sound of the commotion breaking out on all three decks of the *Manatee*—gunshots, shouted curses, yells of pain—Cleghorn's prophecy was already coming true. Longarm returned the grin and clapped Cleghorn on the shoulder as he went by. "Good luck!" he called. "Where's Branch?"

Cleghorn motioned above them with a thumb, then let out a yell and plunged down the steps, waving the bludgeon over his head as he went into battle.

Longarm raced up another companionway to the texas deck. Branch would have left the work of unloading the bullion to the rest of the gang. He would be up in the pilothouse, Longarm thought, keeping an eye on everything and holding O'Brien hostage.

Longarm grabbed a stanchion at the top of the steps and used it as leverage to swing himself around. A bullet whined past his ear as he did so. He looked up and saw Tyler Branch in the big starboard window of the pilothouse. Branch fired again, the slug chewing splinters from the railing around the texas deck. Longarm snapped a shot at him, making him duck back into the shelter of the pilothouse.

"Hold it, Custis!" Branch shouted down to him. "Come any closer and I'll kill O'Brien!"

"Kill the captain and you'll never get off this boat alive!" Longarm called back. "The crew's already breaking loose from your gang, Branch! It's over!"

"The hell it is! We've got the guns!"

Longarm heard the clamor of shots on the lower decks and could tell all the lead wasn't being flung in one direction. "Not all of them, not anymore! There's a battle going on down here, and your boys are losing!"

He hoped that was true. If the bullion gang won, he was going to have a heap of trouble coming up behind him any minute now.

There was silence from the pilothouse. The only way up there was by climbing a narrow ladder. If Longarm tried to go up, Branch could pick him off without any trouble. On the other hand, the ladder was also the only way Branch could escape. It was a true standoff.

That changed dramatically a moment later when a shot sounded in the pilothouse, followed by the violent sounds of a fight. Branch and O'Brien appeared in the window, struggling over the gun. They swayed back and forth for a moment, then surged against the sill and tipped over it. Both men fell, plunging to the texas deck only a few yards from Longarm.

O'Brien landed on the bottom. Longarm heard the sickening snap of a bone breaking. The captain groaned and sprawled motionless on the deck, knocked half-senseless by the fall. Branch had lost his grip on the gun, which slid across the deck boards and came to a stop near Longarm's foot. He bent down and scooped it up as Branch rolled off of O'Brien and came shakily to his feet.

Longarm trained both revolvers on Branch and said, "Now it's really over."

"No!" Branch gasped. "No, damn it! It can't be! We were all going to be rich—"

"We still will be," Estelle Henry said from behind Longarm.

He stiffened and turned his head, saw her at the top of the nearest companionway with a gun in her hand. His heart sank. First Branch, then Glorieta, and now Estelle. All of them really had been in on it. Everyone he had trusted, everyone he had liked, maybe even loved a little . . .

Well, not everyone. Salty hadn't betrayed him. The old pelican was still on his side. But Longarm had left Salty on the bottom deck, standing guard over Glorieta. He couldn't count on the old-timer's help this time.

Keeping the pair of revolvers trained on Branch, Longarm said, "Estelle, you don't want to be doin' this. You haven't killed anybody. If you give it up now, you won't hang. I reckon I can promise you that."

"Nobody's going to hang," Estelle said. "Tyler and Glorieta and I are leaving, and we're taking the bullion with us. Don't make me kill you, Custis. I really don't want to kill you."

Longarm's jaw tightened. "You know, I'm gettin' a mite tired of folks who say they don't want to kill me pointin' guns at me, Stella Jean."

"Don't call me that! It won't do you any good to remind me of the past, Custis. That'll just make me more determined than ever to get that bullion. Once you're poor, you never forget it. Never!" She lifted the pistol and stared over the barrel at him. "Now drop those guns and get out of the way!"

"I'll get him, Estelle!" Branch cried out.

Longarm's head jerked around. He saw the two-barrel, over-and-under derringer appear in Branch's hand, sliding out of a sleeve holster like the one in which he'd kept the dirk on his other arm. Longarm twisted and flung himself

169

down and out of the way as the derringer cracked spite-fully. He often carried a derringer and knew the little guns were inaccurate over a few feet—but deadly at ranges closer than that. He triggered the revolvers as he landed prone on the deck. Twin blasts echoed over the water.

Branch's arm jerked as one of Longarm's slugs ripped through the meat of it. The derringer went flying before Branch could squeeze off the second shot. Branch stumbled backward as Longarm fired again. Both shots missed. Branch writhed around and threw himself toward the rail. Longarm scrambled to his feet and lunged after him, but he was too late. Even wounded, Branch was still lithe and athletic enough to leap to the top of the railing and kick off from it. He sailed out into the air.

Longarm hurried to the rail. It would take one hell of a dive to clear the lower decks and reach the water. But that was exactly what Tyler Branch had just done. He arched out from the boat, aiming for the darker blue of the Colorado's main channel. He hit the water with a splash a few yards from the side of the riverboat, disappearing under the surface.

A groan made Longarm wheel around. He hadn't forgotten about Estelle, but he'd been too busy dodging Branch's lead to worry about her. Now, as he saw her slumped on the deck, he caught his breath. Despite the fact that she had betrayed him and had been deceiving him all along, pain stabbed into him at the thought of her being hurt. He ran to her and went to one knee, setting one of the revolvers aside to grip her shoulder and gently roll her onto her back.

The front of her dress was stained with blood, and her normally fair skin had a deathly pallor to it. Her eyes were open and full of the knowledge of impending death. Longarm knew, looking at her, that when he had thrown himself out of the path of Branch's shot, the bullet had found Estelle instead.

He leaned over and said in a low, urgent voice, "Don't worry, gal. You're going to be all right. I'll get some help, and we'll get you patched right up—"

She stopped his empty reassurances by reaching up and grasping his arm. Her fingers had a clawlike strength. "N-no, Custis," she gasped. "Don't waste time . . . with that . . . just promise me . . . before it's too late . . . promise me . . ."

"What is it?" he asked. "What is it you want?"

"Promise me . . . you won't hurt . . . Tyler . . ."

Longarm's mouth tightened into a bleak line. How could he make a promise like that when Branch was a killer and an outlaw, the leader of a gang responsible for dozens of cold-blooded murders?

"I'm a lawman, Estelle," he began. "I have to go after him—"

"No!" The word was a wail of mortal pain as it came from Estelle's mouth. "You don't . . . understand! You can't kill him, Custis, because . . . he's my son . . ." Her hand slipped off his arm as the last of her strength began to desert her. "My son . . . and yours . . ."

Chapter 13

For a moment, the world spun crazily around Longarm. He couldn't think, couldn't make sense of what Estelle had just told him, couldn't even begin to comprehend what she had said. But then his thoughts cleared, and as he looked down at her, he felt nothing but pure, heart-breaking regret.

"That last time . . . we were together . . . made a baby," she whispered. "When Tyler was born . . . I tried to find you . . . but you'd gone off to the war. . . . I never thought I'd see you again . . ." Incredibly, she smiled through her pain. Her hand touched his arm again, but this time it was a caress of farewell. "So glad," she murmured. "So glad we found each other . . . one more . . . last time . . ."

With that, the life went out of her eyes. She stared up sightlessly at the blue Arizona sky.

Longarm drew in a deep, ragged breath and climbed to his feet. He pushed the grief he felt at Estelle's death far into the back of his mind, next to the shock and sorrow he'd experienced when he realized she was in league with the bullion gang. The jumble of emotions that had gone through him when Estelle said that Tyler Branch was his son was back there, too. He couldn't afford to let himself feel too much right now, not when he still had a job to do. He had to think instead.

He tucked the extra pistol behind his belt and holstered his Colt as he went to check on Captain O'Brien. The captain was unconscious, and the odd way his left arm was bent told Longarm it was broken. But O'Brien was breathing regularly and Longarm figured he was just knocked out.

Straightening, Longarm looked out across the river. There was no sign of Tyler Branch swimming toward either bank. Had he drowned when he went under? Or had he already reached the shore and gotten away?

Footsteps pounded on the companionway. Longarm spun around, his hand reaching for the butt of his revolver. Joe Cleghorn and Jerome Horton appeared at the top of the steps. Cleghorn still had the length of wood in his hand, while Horton was carrying a pistol. Both men were disheveled and bloody, but they didn't seem to be hurt too badly. Cleghorn saw O'Brien lying there and exclaimed, "Cap'n!"

"I think he's all right," Longarm said. "His arm's busted and he got knocked cold when he fell out of the pilothouse, but he's breathing."

Cleghorn hurried past, saying, "I'll tend to him. Won't be the first time the cap'n's been bunged up in a fight. Why, one time in Macao . . ."

"Where's Glorieta?" Horton asked anxiously as he came up to Longarm, interrupting Cleghorn's reminiscence.

Longarm didn't answer right away. Instead, he asked a question of his own. "Is the ruckus down below over?"

Horton nodded. "When the shooting started, the passengers and crew were able to jump some of the gang and get their guns. Cleghorn grabbed that chunk of wood and was a holy terror with it. Some of the raiders are dead, and the others are all prisoners with the crew and passengers guarding them. But I can't find Glorieta anywhere. What the hell's going on, Long? Where is she?"

Longarm hesitated before answering. "Tyler Branch was behind all of it, Horton. He's been running the gang all along." He took a deep breath. "And Glorieta was part of it with him. She's the one who's been supplying information to the gang about the bullion shipments."

Horton's blood-streaked features turned ashen. "No! My God, that's not possible!"

"She was in on it," Longarm said again. He pointed to the lifeless form lying on the deck a few feet away. "And so was Estelle." He didn't say anything about Estelle's claim that Branch was really his son.

Horton dropped the pistol in his coat pocket and put his hands over his face. He started to sob. The gang that had been plaguing him, that had threatened to ruin him, had been broken up, but the rest of his dreams had been shattered. Longarm didn't blame the man for crying. If Longarm had been the sort, he might have shed a few tears himself on this tragic day.

Finally, Horton lowered his hands and asked, "Where . . . where is she? Was she hurt?"

"Just knocked out," Longarm assured him. "I left her down on the bottom deck with Salty guarding her."

"I . . . I have to go to her." Horton started to turn away.

Longarm stopped him by saying, "Horton. Don't get any ideas about turning her loose. She's under arrest."

"I know," Horton said heavily. "I just have to . . . to see her again."

Longarm turned back to Cleghorn and O'Brien as Horton hurried below. The captain was conscious now, and Cleghorn had him propped up against the wall. O'Brien was gray-faced from the pain of his broken arm, but his gaze was alert as he said, "Long, are you all right? Is everything under control?"

"Yep to both questions," Longarm told him.

"What about Branch?"

Longarm shook his head. "I ain't sure about him yet. He might've got away, or he might have drowned when he dived in the river—"

Movement on shore caught Longarm's eye. He saw a flash of red as he peered toward the bluffs that lined the Colorado.

Stiffening, he asked O'Brien, "Field glasses in the pilothouse?"

"Aye. What—"

But Longarm was gone already, scrambling up the ladder to the tiny structure perched at the highest level of the riverboat.

He found the glasses, snatched them up, and leaned out the window. Bringing the glasses to his eyes, he focused them on the shore. Figures sprang into sharp relief as he squinted through the lenses. He saw Tyler Branch and Glorieta McCall, mounted on a couple of the horses belonging to the gang. They were making their way up a trail that led to the top of the bluff. Even at this distance, Longarm could tell that their clothes were soaked and plastered to their bodies. Branch had been able to swim to shore, and somehow, Glorieta had managed to do the same thing.

Longarm dropped the glasses and hurried out of the pilothouse to climb down the ladder. A horrible feeling was growing inside him. He had left Salty watching over Glorieta, and now she was loose again. What had happened to the old man?

Clattering down the companionways, Longarm reached the bottom deck and ran along it until he came to the spot where Jerome Horton was helping a groggy-looking Salty to his feet. Longarm gripped Salty's arm and asked, "Are you all right?"

"Other than feelin' like a damn-blasted old fool!" Salty said as he took off his hat and rubbed his head. "I took my eyes off that gal for one second, and she walloped me! Knocked my lights right out! Where'd she go, anyway?"

"Jumped overboard and swam ashore," Longarm replied grimly. "Just like Branch." He pointed toward the bluff on the east side of the Colorado. "If you look right quick, you might see both of 'em goin' over the top of that rise over yonder."

"Then they've escaped," Horton said. "At least they didn't get away with any of the bullion."

"No," Longarm said, "and they haven't gotten away yet, either."

Horton and Salty looked at him. "What do you mean?" Horton asked.

"I mean I'm going after them. My job ain't over."

Salty insisted on going along, and nothing Longarm could say would persuade him otherwise. "I got a stake in this, too," the old-timer declared. "The gal clouted me just like she clouted you, Custis. Besides, I know this part o' the country like the back o' my hand. Did a bit o' prospectin' down here before I went to drivin' stagecoaches and freight wagons."

"All right," Longarm said. He didn't have time to argue.

He had gathered up some extra ammunition and supplies already. He hoped to be able to catch a couple of the gang's horses when he and Salty got ashore. Joe Cleghorn had a boat ready to shove off. Cleghorn had a bandage wrapped around his head and several others around his torso, but he took the oars himself as Longarm and Salty climbed into the boat.

"You'll be taking the *Manatee* back downriver to Yuma?" Longarm asked as Cleghorn began to row toward shore.

"That's right. Between Cap'n O'Brien and me, we're

in good enough shape to handle things. We'll turn those outlaws over to the sheriff when we get there. Anything else you need me to do, Long?"

"Send a wire to my boss, Chief Marshal Billy Vail in Denver, and tell him that I've gone after Branch and the girl. I'll report in to him as soon as I can."

Cleghorn looked at Longarm through narrowed eyes. "How come you're so determined to catch up with that bucko? His gang's busted all to hell."

"The job's not over until Branch is in custody or dead," Longarm said. He tried not to think about what Estelle had told him. He could mull over all of that later.

He hadn't given his promise. That knowledge gnawed at him. He hadn't promised Estelle that he wouldn't hurt Branch.

But could he bring himself to do it? Could he gun down his own son if Branch put up a fight?

Longarm kept his eyes on the approaching shore and told himself not to try to make that decision now. Maybe it wouldn't come to that.

A short time later, the hull of the boat scraped on the sandy riverbank. Longarm and Salty climbed out of the little vessel. "I'll keep the *Manatee* anchored there in the middle of the stream until I'm sure you've been able to catch some horses. You don't want to be stranded out here."

Longarm nodded his thanks. He was carrying a canvas bag filled with the supplies and spare cartridges. He slung it over his shoulder and strode away from the river without looking back. Salty followed, hurrying a little to catch up.

"Where you reckon them horses'll be?" the old-timer asked.

"Somewhere close by unless Branch stampeded all of them," Longarm replied. He led the way through some boulders that had been washed downriver in previous floods, to be deposited in a mazelike fashion on the shore. As he and Salty trudged on, he heard what he'd been hoping to hear: horses blowing and stamping.

Longarm came around a boulder and saw half a dozen horses picketed only a few yards away. Branch and Glorieta had been in too much of a hurry to turn the other animals loose. They had just grabbed a couple of mounts and taken off up the trail. Now Longarm and Salty selected the strongest looking of the remaining horses and freed the others. They would find their way back to civilization eventually, either to Hardyville or La Paz.

"Where do you reckon them two will head?" Salty asked.

Longarm knew he was talking about Branch and Glorieta. "The girl said they were going to Mexico, but that was when she thought they were going to get away with the bullion."

"They've prob'ly got the loot from the other holdups stashed somewhere," Salty pointed out.

Longarm nodded in agreement. "I figure they'll try to get to it, then head for the border if they can. Right now, though, they're just trying to put some distance between themselves and the river. I want to catch up to them before they can get to their hideout."

"Chances are some o' the ones who got took prisoner back on the boat will spill the location of the hidin' place."

"That's just one more reason for Branch to hurry. He'll want to get there before the law has a chance to. I wonder how much he knows about getting along in this part of the country."

Salty pulled at his beard and frowned in thought. "He's been full o' surprises so far, that's for sure."

"Him and the gal, both," Longarm said.

"Yeah."

They reached the top of the bluff and halted to look

back at the river. Longarm saw Joe Cleghorn standing on the texas deck, watching. He took off his Stetson and waved it over his head, signaling to Cleghorn that the *Manatee* could pull up anchor and start downriver again. Then he and Salty turned and rode east.

They came out on level ground that ran for several miles before some foothills popped up. Beyond the foothills was a range of rugged, rounded peaks.

"Those are the Castle Dome Mountains," Salty said. "I've been through 'em a time or two. There's a good pass, but it ain't that easy to get to. If Branch knows about it, that's where he'll head."

"Glorieta told me he had scouted the river a couple of times. I reckon there's a good chance he knows about that pass."

"So we head for it?" Salty said grimly.

Longarm nodded. "We do."

"I'll lead the way." Salty heeled his horse into a lope. Longarm fell in alongside him. The ground was too hard to take many tracks, but he kept his eyes open for them anyway, just in case. He was a pretty good tracker.

They rode through the day, reaching the foothills and winding through them toward the mountains. By late afternoon, the Castle Domes were looming above them. Longarm's eyes searched the range of mountains for the pass that Salty had mentioned, but he didn't see it. In fact, the terrain was getting more rugged and challenging, forcing them to move at a slower pace.

"Dadgum it!" Salty said as the blazing orb of the sun began to sink below the western horizon, far behind them. "I don't know if we're goin' to find 'em or not."

"I reckon we will," Longarm said, reining in and pointing at something he'd just seen. "Look up yonder."

Shadows were beginning to cloak the mountains. In the gathering gloom, a small, winking speck of red light was visible.

"A campfire," Salty breathed. "They stopped and built a campfire."

A chilly wind swirled through the foothills. "The girl probably got cold," Longarm said. "And Branch likely figures we're still on that riverboat." Longarm leaned forward in the saddle. "He should've known better."

Salty looked over at him and said slowly, "Yeah, you ain't one to give up, are you, Custis?"

"Not hardly. Not when there's a job to do."

"That's what I figured . . ." Salty gave a little shake of his head, as if coming out of a reverie. "I reckon you're goin' up there?"

"That's right. Are you comin' with me?"

"Damn right I am." Salty heeled his horse into motion. "Let's go."

Night fell, and still the two men climbed higher into the mountains. The horses were surefooted, and Longarm was thankful for that. Their path twisted and turned, and sometimes they could no longer see the campfire above them. But then it came into view again, and they forged on.

Finally, when Longarm estimated they were about half a mile from the spot, he reined in and dismounted. Salty followed suit. "We'll go ahead on foot," Longarm said quietly. "And keep that hogleg of yours handy. I don't trust Branch not to have set up some sort of ambush. That gang of his did that before."

"I ain't forgot," Salty said, sounding disgruntled. "You ever stop to think, maybe that ain't them up yonder? Could be a prospector or a trapper built that fire?"

"Maybe so," Longarm said. "If it turns out that way, we'll try to pick up their trail in the morning. It'll be harder, but I ain't turnin' back."

"Nope. Never thought you would."

They moved quietly up the slope and came out on a shoulder of land that jutted out from the side of a mountain. A couple of hundred yards away, the campfire flickered under some stubby pine trees. Longarm moved closer, Salty shadowing him. Longarm's keen eyes recognized Tyler Branch and Glorieta McCall huddling next to the fire. In this high, arid country, all the heat of the day vanished almost as soon as the sun went down, and the air grew cold. Longarm's breath fogged in front of his face. The heat from that fire probably felt mighty good to those fugitives. It was going to prove their undoing, though.

Longarm stopped and turned to Salty. He motioned to the left. "Circle around that way," he whispered. "I'll head to the right. We'll have them in a cross fire if it comes to that."

Salty nodded. He slipped off silently into the darkness.

Longarm angled to the right, skirting the trees and coming in toward the camp from the south. He had learned over the years how to move in near-total silence when he had to, and this was one of those times. He dropped to hands and knees for the final approach, standing up again only when he was almost to the outer limits of the circle of light cast by the fire. He drew his gun and stepped forward. Branch was sitting with his back to him, and Longarm centered the sights on the outlaw.

His son.

Don't think about that. Just arrest him, like you've arrested a hundred other desperadoes.

He moved into the light. Glorieta saw him and gasped. As Branch started to his feet, Longarm called, "Don't move! There's a gun pointing right at your back, Branch!"

That would be Salty's signal to move in from the other side. But as Branch crouched there stiffly and Longarm kept him covered, the old man failed to appear. Longarm wondered where the hell he was, but there was no time to find out now.

"Custis?" Branch said without turning around. "You came after me? Really?"

"What else did you expect? You go after what you want, don't you, Branch?" Longarm's voice shook a little. "They say the apple don't fall far from the tree."

"What? What the hell are you talking about?"

Despite all his good intentions, Longarm couldn't stop the words that spilled from him. "Estelle told me all about it. She told me that you were her son."

"What? That's insane! We made a good team, but that was all." Branch laughed. "Still, she was almost like a mother to me. She taught me everything I know."

Longarm frowned. "What are you sayin'? She wasn't your mother?"

"Of course not. We met a couple of years ago on the Mississippi, on a riverboat."

"And your father?" Longarm asked.

"Claxton Tillotson Branch, the headmaster of a boy's school in St. Louis. The biggest bastard in the world. That's why I ran away when I was fifteen and started making my own way on the river. You can verify all that, Custis, if you want to go to that much trouble. Though why you'd want to is beyond me."

Longarm's voice was hoarse with emotion as he said, "Then why would Estelle say such a thing? Why would she claim you were her son?" Longarm didn't say anything about the rest of her claim.

For the first time, Glorieta spoke up. "Because she was insane, just like Tyler said! She couldn't have children, never could! She told me all about it, when she wasn't busy slipping into your cabin. You were her first and only love, Custis. She was a damned fool." Glorieta shot to her feet. "And so are you!"

Her hand came out of the folds of her dress and she lifted a gun. She pointed it past Branch at Longarm. "Drop it!" she cried.

Longarm hesitated. Branch laughed. "My hand is on my gun, Custis," he said. "If you try to get Glorieta, I'll spin around and drop you before you can switch your aim back to me. I'm fast enough and good enough to do it, I promise you. But if you shoot me, she'll shoot you. So what are you going to do, Custis? Stand there and die?"

At last, Salty stepped out of the shadows behind Glorieta. The barrel of the heavy revolver in his hand prodded the center of her back. "Nobody has to die," the old-timer rasped. "Drop the gun, gal."

Glorieta's eyes widened in surprise. She fired, but Longarm was already throwing himself to the side. At the same time, Branch whirled around and drew his gun, his speed as blinding as he had boasted. Glorieta's bullet whipped past Longarm's head while the slug from Branch's gun thudded into the trunk of one of the pines. On one knee, Longarm fired twice. Both bullets ripped through Branch's body. He cried out in pain as the impact of the lead spun him around and dropped him to the ground.

Salty chopped at Glorieta's arm with the gun in his hand, cracking the barrel across her wrist. She dropped the gun and stumbled forward, falling to her knees.

On the other side of the fire, Branch writhed as the life bled out of him. Longarm approached him carefully, keeping the Colt trained on him. Branch shuddered and then lay still, but he wasn't quite dead yet. He stared up at Longarm as a ghastly grin stretched across his face. "If you thought Estelle . . . was my mother, Custis . . . then who did you think . . . was my father?"

He started to laugh, but the sound turned into a death rattle.

Longarm regarded him bleakly for a moment, then holstered his Colt. He felt a vast sense of relief mixed with sadness, and he didn't want to ponder too much on what had caused both of those emotions. He said, "I reckon that's the end of it. We'll take the girl back to Yuma, Salty."

"No," Salty said. "We won't."

Longarm looked up and met the old man's determined eyes. "What did you say?"

"I said we ain't takin' the girl back to Yuma," Salty declared. "She's gonna get on one o' those horses and ride away, and ain't nobody goin' after her."

Understanding began to filter into Longarm's brain as he recalled some of the things that had been said to him by both Salty and Glorieta. "Back on the boat, you gave her the chance to get away on purpose, didn't you?"

Salty nodded. "I had to, once I saw the picture in that locket she stomped. I wish she'd stoved my head in, though, instead o' just knockin' me out. Then I never would've had to make the decision I got to make now." His voice shook. "But I can't let you take my little girl to jail, Custis. I just can't."

Kneeling in front of the old man with her back to him, Glorieta turned her head to peer up at him in amazement. "Your . . . little girl?" she repeated.

Tears ran down Salty's leathery old cheeks as he said, "That's right. That was your mama's picture in that locket. I heard you pretty near say as much. And she was my wife, back in the days when I was still prospectin'. She left me when she couldn't stand that life, and she never told me she was with child. Then when I heard you tellin' Custis about what happened to her after that . . . and what happened to you . . . I knew I had to do what I could for you."

"You?" Glorieta whispered. "*You* were my father?"

"Still am," Salty said. "Now you go on. Get out o' here, and don't never come back to this part o' the country. Find yourself a good man and settle down, and put all this thievin' and outlawry behind you. Do it for me, gal. Do it for your old pa."

185

"All . . . all right," Glorieta said, her voice choked with emotion. "I'll do it." She put a hand on the ground in front of her to balance herself as she started to get to her feet.

"Salty, look out!" Longarm yelled as he saw Glorieta's hand dart toward the pistol she had dropped a few minutes earlier.

Salty didn't fire his gun, though he could have. He stepped back, stunned by his daughter's act of treachery. Glorieta had the gun in her hand and snapped a shot at him, hitting him and driving him back, out of her way. Longarm had drawn his Colt by now, but Glorieta jerked out of the way as he triggered the revolver. She broke into a run, leaping past Salty's fallen form and vanishing into the darkness.

Salty twisted around on the ground and held out a hand after her, as if he could catch her and pull her back. "No!" he cried. "Glorieta, no! Don't run off that way!"

Longarm started after her, but he stopped short as a scream suddenly tore through the night. It was a scream of terror, and it was cut off abruptly by an ugly thud.

"Help me!" Salty said frantically to Longarm. "Help me up!"

Longarm grabbed the old man's arm and hauled him to his feet, then stooped to snatch a burning brand from the campfire as Salty stumbled off in the direction Glorieta had gone. Using the brand as a torch, Longarm hurried after him and found him a moment later standing on the edge of a ravine that slashed across the shoulder of ground. The drop was a sheer one of twenty feet or more. Longarm stepped up beside Salty, and the light from the makeshift torch in his hand spilled down into the declivity to reveal Glorieta lying at the bottom, her head twisted grotesquely on her neck. The flames reflected back from her dead, glassy eyes.

"I knew the ravine was here," Salty choked out as he

186

used his right hand to clutch at the new bullet wound in his left upper arm. "That's what slowed me down when I was circlin' the camp. I had to go around it. I tried to stop her, Custis."

"I know you did," Longarm said quietly. "You tried to do your very best for her, Salty."

"I never knowed who she was until today. I swear I never did."

"I believe you."

"But I broke the law anyway, by tryin' to help her get away. I even tried to lead you off the trail, in hopes you'd give up." Salty sighed. "I reckon you got to arrest me now, Custis. It's the right thing to do."

Longarm thought about everything that had happened: about how Don Hernando Aragones had lost a son; about how he himself had gained—and lost—a son he'd never really had; and about how this old pelican beside him had gained—and lost forever—a daughter he had never really known.

Then he tossed the torch down into the ravine to let it gutter out among the rocks and said, "Right or wrong, sometimes the only thing to do is to try to forget."

Watch for

LONGARM AND THE SINFUL SISTERS

295th novel in the exciting
LONGARM series from Jove

Coming in June!